THE ITALIAN CONNECTION

Junior writer Megan fears she has taken on too much when she accepts a magazine travel assignment in Italy. Yet as she copes with setbacks and shares her experiences with her new online followers, her confidence grows — along with her love for the beautiful country, and her feelings for brooding olive farmer Giovanni. But will her jealous, spiteful colleague Anna ruin everything?

ELIZABETH McGINTY

THE ITALIAN CONNECTION

Complete and Unabridged

LINFORD
Leicester

First published in Great Britain in 2022

First Linford Edition
published 2023

A catalogue record for this book is available
from the British Library.

ISBN 978–1–4448–5110–6

Published by
Ulverscroft Limited
Anstey, Leicestershire

Printed and bound in Great Britain by
TJ Books Ltd., Padstow, Cornwall

This book is printed on acid-free paper

1

Megan squinted through the corridor window, watching out for her editor, Bob, who would be demanding her article in the next few minutes. She hated this part of her job, never sure whether her words would be good enough or that she had captured the correct perspective.

Out of the corner of her eye she could see him scouring the room looking for her. She knew she had to return to the main office and face her fear.

'Ah, Megan there you are, is your article ready for a final read through?' Bob asked in his gruff voice, which still made her jump even though she had worked with him for five years and knew he was at heart a very kindly man.

'Yes sir, all ready.'

'Good — bring it into my office and I'll read it now,' Bob instructed.

Megan bit her lip as she stood in front of the desk, waiting, as he read.

'Well,' Bob eventually said. 'It's a fine article. Well done, our advertisers will love it. Please sit down.'

'Thank you, sir.' She sat gingerly on the edge of the seat nearest to her.

'You're a good writer, Megan, especially your travel reports. You bring the world alive. It's a skill few possess,' Bob continued. Megan felt a blush rise in her face. 'Did you know the magazine is considering options for a big project in Italy?'

'I had heard, sir.'

'I think you could be just the person.'

'Me, sir?' She was flabbergasted.

'Do you not think you're up to it? I seem to remember you are quite fluent in languages. Is Italian one of them?'

Megan took a short breath as she searched for a response. She didn't want Bob to think she had no faith in her own skill, but she could feel her stomach flutter at the enormity of the task.

'Yes, I can get by in Italian, and French and Spanish . . .' Then she came back down to earth. 'It's not that, sir, I just wondered if there weren't longer serving

2

staff in the team, who might be expecting the project to be theirs.'

'I hope you aren't questioning my decision-making?' Bob said, but there was a hint of a smile on his face. 'Give it some thought. It's your project if you want it, but I need your answer by Monday.' He turned his attention back to work on his desk. 'Oh, and Megan, please call me Bob.'

'Thank you, sir, I mean Bob, thank you.'

Megan left the office, her heart pounding with excitement. Bob thought she was good enough to be given the responsibility of this huge piece of work.

It was dark as she left the office and the icy January wind made her pull her scarf close around her as she made her way to her car. The discussion with Bob was still ringing in her head and she tried to balance feelings of excitement and fear. It was a big risk. If she failed, her career would be over, but if she succeeded . . . well, who knew what the future held? She only had the weekend to make the decision. Tonight, she would curl up on the sofa in the flat she shared with her sister, with a takeaway and a glass of prosecco while she considered her options and imagined what her life would be like if she accepted the opportunity of spending a summer in Italy.

Maybe it was because her mind was distracted, but she didn't hear the two men in the car park until it was too late. As she rounded the corner suddenly there they were in front of her, causing her to almost jump out of her skin.

The taller of the two clearly sensed her anxiety and stepped back apologising, allowing her to pass. When she reached her car she was shaking, and dropped her handbag in her haste.

'Here, let me,' a male voice said.

Megan jumped again, but as she looked up, the dark-haired stranger stood before her holding her car keys, which had fallen out of her bag.

'Your keys. Are you OK? I apologise if my brother and I startled you.'

The question was gentle, the brown

eyes soft and concerned. His voice held an accent.

'Yes, I'm OK —' Megan began to speak then realised her tone was sharp. Taking a deep breath, she softened it. 'Yes, thank you, just distracted.' She accepted the keys held out to her.

'OK, then, if you're sure.'

He moved away to let her open her car door, then as Megan checked in her rear-view mirror, she saw him continue to watch until she had driven out of the car park.

★   ★   ★

Megan should have guessed her sister, Chloe, would be suspicious when she brought home takeaway food, before pay day at the end of the month.

'Oh my word, Megan, it's the chance of a lifetime and the opportunity to showcase your writing to a bigger audience!' Chloe said when Megan told her of Bob's offer. 'What are you even considering?'

Chloe was a professional athlete and seized every opportunity that came her way.

'It is, Chloe, I'm so astonished to be offered this project and my head is buzzing with ideas already. I'd never have believed, when I moved to London from Little Budlow, that I would be given this opportunity.'

'So, what's the problem? You know I believe in making things happen and grabbing every chance you're offered.'

'My lack of experience, for one thing.' Megan kept her head down. 'I mean, I almost fainted when two strange men spoke to me in the car park. How will I cope alone in a strange country?'

She described to Chloe how she had dropped her handbag in the car park and then, when she returned home, discovering that her favourite keyring had broken off which carried an old childhood photo of her and her dog. She felt her face flush as she remembered the kindly face of the stranger who tried to help her.

Chloe made a noise that could have been caused by the spices in her food catching the back of her throat, but Megan suspected it was more along the lines of dismissing Megan's fears.

After a moment's silence and a drink of water, Chloe took a deep breath and spoke softly.

'Megan, you are my sister and I love you dearly but I need to say my piece. Whether you take it on board or not is entirely up to you and I will support you whatever you choose. I think you need to take this opportunity, and I think if the shoe was on the other foot you would push me to seize the chance with both hands. And you, my darling adorable sister, would support me every step of the way.' She continued, 'Now open that bottle of fizz so I can celebrate my talented sister, before I have to hit the gym in the morning to work it all off. And tell me more about these gallant gentlemen who make you blush when you talk about them.'

She held her glass aloft, laughing.

When Megan awoke in the morning, for a few minutes she envisioned herself living life in Florence or Rome or Venice with the warm Italian sunshine playing on her shoulders . . . the smell of fresh coffee and authentic pizza . . . and the sound of sultry Italian voices filling her ears.

With a jolt, she jumped up, remembering the man from the car park. He was Italian — why hadn't she realised before? Could this be the sign she needed to help make her decision?

★　★　★

Megan heard Chloe's key in the lock as she sat in the lounge with an unfinished mug of tea, long gone cold, in her hands.

'Helloooo,' Chloe called from the hallway. 'I'm gasping for a cuppa. Do you want one too? Then I'll make a start on dinner. Are you eating in? I'm thinking pasta with Italian sausage.'

'I'm not hungry, and I've decided I'm not going to take the job,' Megan said.

All her confidence from the night before had disappeared.

'Fine — that's your choice.' Chloe began unpacking her shopping bags.

'It's too far away, for too long, it's just too much,' Megan said, moving into the kitchen to make fresh tea for them both.

'And too Italian, too picturesque, too much the opportunity of a lifetime, I dare say,' Chloe continued. 'I remember when you used to make positive decisions, like dumping that waster of a boyfriend who tried to hold you back in your career. I wonder where that girl disappeared to?'

'Oh, Chloe, what a lucky escape that was. He was such a shallow social climber.' Megan made a face at her sister. 'Maybe I was less fearful then. What if this goes wrong and I lose my job?'

'Bob wouldn't have considered offering it to you, if he didn't trust you to give it your best shot, and what on earth could you possibly do that would result in being sacked?' Chloe said. 'Now drink your tea, while I prepare dinner.'

Eventually the tantalising smell from

the kitchen tempted Megan back to the table. Despite her protestations of her lack of appetite, she enjoyed the delicious meal. She even smiled as her sister plonked a bottle of red wine on the table.

'I reckon we deserve this.' Chloe smiled back.

'Well, you do, Chloe. Thank you so much for being a fantastic big sister and looking after me.'

'You would do the same for me.' Chloe reached over to clink glasses with Megan. 'To us.'

'Yes, to us,' Megan said with less enthusiasm. 'Do you think Mum and Dad will be happy if I take the project? I won't be able to pop back home and see them while I'm away.'

'Of course, Megan, they want you to be happy and they will be very proud of you. But this is about pleasing you, not other people. However I definitely know someone who will be delighted if you accept the project.'

'I can't imagine who else would be delighted. I know you are pleased because you will get the place to yourself, which does worry me, I must admit. Who will be here to keep an eye on you?'

'I knew you'd try to play the I-can't-leave-you-in-this-big-flat-on-your-own-so-far-away-from-family card.' Chloe laughed.

'You know me well.'

'And that is why I have arranged for a new flatmate to move in.'

'What? I can't believe you've done that before I've even made up my mind.' Megan put down her glass and added crossly, 'And you've been off making arrangements with one of your friends.'

'It's not a friend.'

'Well that's worse, I don't want a stranger living in my room when I'm not here. I'd sooner leave it empty. I will still be paying my share after all.'

Chloe laughed. 'And this is the girl who declared she wasn't going. Oh Megan, my new flatmate is our brother. He's been talking about moving to London on a secondment with the Met. He asked if he could move in with us on a temporary basis — with him studying fashion design he wants to test the opportunities for him here.'

'Oh, that's good news, I'm pleased for him.'

'So, are you going to match his ambition?' Chloe asked.

Megan smiled broadly and hugged her sister.

'How can I not?'

* * *

It was with trepidation that Megan made her way to work on Monday morning, her bravado over taking on the project diluted in the face of the huge weight being placed on her shoulders and whether she did indeed have the skills and talent to do the magazine and herself justice.

'Take a seat, Megan.' Bob shuffled folders on his desk, searching for the one he wanted. 'Now about this project — there's been a development.'

Megan felt her mouth go dry and

prepared herself to accept bad news graciously.

'I am going on the assumption that you have thought this over and accepted the assignment. So, I would expect you to be ready to leave for Italy next week.' Bob looked at her for confirmation.

Megan must have managed a nod as Bob continued. 'I have a folder somewhere with all the travel and accommodation arrangements. But there's been a change of plan. Our publishing group has decided to make this a joint project with one of our sister magazines based in Verona — killing two birds with one stone, as it were — and Claudia, the editor, is arranging for you to be joined on the project by one of their photographers.'

Megan realised Bob was expecting a response.

'That won't be a problem.' Megan had no idea whether it would be a problem — she had no experience to judge against. 'Thank you, Bob — I am really grateful to be given this opportunity.'

Bob laughed, a deep jovial laugh. 'I hope you still feel like that when you are bombarded with deadlines to meet, have spent days on the road and the weather is too hot, and there are too many tourists to get the story you want.'

Megan gulped. 'I'll do my very best, Bob. I won't let you down.'

'I'm sure you won't, Megan. Now this photographer was due to meet us here this morning —' As he spoke the telephone rang and Bob answered with a gruff, 'Hello — right, thank you, send him in.' He turned to Megan. 'It seems our chap has arrived.'

Megan's mind was in a whirl trying to decide if she really could work with a stranger for the next few months, and a male stranger at that. She looked up trying to put her most confident smile in place to greet her new work partner.

Bob's assistant opened the door and announced, 'Luca Rossi for you, sir.'

Megan heard herself gasp as she recognised one of the men from the car park.

'Hello again.' Luca smiled, reaching

into his pocket. 'What a surprise. I believe I have something belonging to you.' He handed a small tissue-wrapped object to Megan.

She unwrapped it, aware of Bob's eyes on her, and smiled broadly as she saw Rufus' photo in her lost keyring.

'Oh! Thank you. I thought it was lost forever.'

Luca smiled back. 'My friend has posted it on social media to try to track you down, but now I can tell her I have found you.'

Megan's mood swung between delight that her photo had been found and terror that she would be working with this sophisticated Italian man.

Bob coughed. 'I take it you know each other.'

'No,' they both exclaimed simultaneously.

'Sorry, sir.' Megan explained. 'We bumped into each other as I was leaving the office on Friday, when I dropped my bag, and this gentleman, sorry Luca, retrieved my keys. I must have lost this in the process. I carry it with me for good luck.'

'I cannot take the credit, it was my brother Giovanni, who is in the UK on a business trip, he found the key ring. He has a dog not unlike the one in the photo. He will be delighted you have been found.' Luca smiled.

Megan blushed. She desperately wanted both men to treat her as a serious professional, so she decided it would be best to give no further explanation. She stopped speaking and waited for Bob to give further instructions.

Before long, all the travel details were in place. It was agreed Megan would leave for Italy the following week and would link up with Luca in Verona to begin work at the offices of Piccolo Mondo, the partner magazine for the project. Luca, it transpired, was a free-lance photographer.

Megan's enthusiasm for the project gave her the courage to make a suggestion to Bob.

'Have you considered a daily update

on social media and a blog, maybe something like *Girl On Tour*?' She described the outline of her idea and how it could engage the readers more.

'Brilliant, Megan.' Bob beamed. 'I knew you were the correct choice for this project, and you doubted my wisdom.' He laughed.

Luca smiled. Megan didn't know if it was meant to be encouraging or condescending. Her judgment of men was often way off the mark.

'Of course,' Bob went on, 'accommodation during your travel across Italy is arranged, but it might be good to have a base in Verona.'

'I could help with that,' Luca offered.

Megan felt horrified. Was he going to suggest she moved in with him?

Luca smiled again as if he knew her thoughts.

'My sister has a spare bedroom in her apartment. Her friend has recently moved out.'

'Sounds ideal,' Bob said. 'Does that suit you, Megan?'

She did not wish to be under obligation to this stranger or be in a situation where a colleague could drop in unannounced, but couldn't explain her opinion in words that would not sound churlish or ungrateful and so she agreed it sounded ideal.

'Good.' Luca smiled.

By the end of the working day Megan's head was bursting with details and throbbing from too much caffeine. Luca had left to catch the same flight home as his brother, and Bob had left Megan to arrange the handover of anything she had been working on to her team.

She drove home with mixed feelings of excitement, exhaustion and trepidation at the enormity of the task in front of her. Why, oh why, had she added to her workload by offering to update social media on a daily basis?

Then there was the complication of sharing a flat with the sister of her new colleague, whom she had realised was also the sister of the handsome Giovanni, causing even more turmoil in her head.

2

Megan checked and rechecked her boarding pass for the Verona flight. Yes, it was for Megan Hopkins. She laughed at herself, behaving as though she had never flown before.

The situation was both liberating and frightening. She decided this would be a good starting point for her travelogue. She wondered how she would be able to produce enough material, especially considering the length of time taken to come up with a title for the blog. Eventually they had settled on *From Pizza To Pisa*.

On her final catch-up in the offices of Oyster World, Bob had explained that she was being allocated a prepaid travel card to cover any purchases not already paid by the company, or where she needed cash, and that it would be topped up whenever necessary.

Her brother Ryan, with his police

background, lectured her on keeping herself and her possessions safe.

Considering Ryan's horrific tales, it came as a relief to find her parents were delighted at the opportunity. Although they had concerns and muttered warnings, they trusted her to make the correct decisions. They had been equally understanding and sympathetic about her broken engagement but didn't seem too surprised.

Now waiting in the bustle of the airport for the call to board her flight, she shivered with excitement. With her back to the window, she raised her newly acquired company mobile phone to take a selfie with the plane in the background. Before her confidence left her, she downloaded the image to the Pizza To Pisa Instagram, Twitter and Facebook accounts set up for her by Tracey. *Look out Italy, here comes Megan*, she tagged the photo and quickly hit send. She smiled as she realised, with a sense of relief, that no one had paid the slightest bit of attention to her actions.

* * *

It seemed to Megan that from the moment the plane touched down, she entered an entirely different world, inhabited by self-assured men and women who were not only confident in their body language but also stylishly dressed.

She wished her brother Ryan had spent more time discussing Italian fashion with her than scaring the wits out of her. At least he had gifted her one of his individually designed scarves to lift her unadventurous wardrobe.

Looking around at these beautifully dressed women, she could see how talented her brother was and wondered whether she would ever be able to exude such an air of confidence herself.

Excitement coursed through her even as she collected her luggage from the carousel and made her way through the airport, searching for the driver whom the email from Piccolo Mondo advised would be there to meet her.

She scanned the arrivals area for someone holding up a sign, as she had seen in films. It took her by surprise to hear someone call her name. Her surprise turned to shock when she realised it was Luca. He stood before her, smiling.

'Hello Megan, welcome to Italy. I can tell you were not expecting to be greeted by me.' He smiled and reached forward, placing a kiss on either side of her face.

Even in her confusion Megan registered how gorgeous he smelled. She suddenly became aware she maybe didn't smell quite so fresh after being confined in a plane for the last few hours.

'Claudia thought it would be better for me to greet you when your plane landed as I already know you. She has a full diary of meetings this morning and has suggested we drop your luggage off at the flat, have lunch and then go into the office to meet up with her and the other staff. Does that suit you?'

'Of course, I'm happy to fall in with whatever plans have been made.'

Luca smiled as he helped with her luggage. 'I hope Verona does not disappoint you, Megan.'

'I hope I don't disappoint Verona.' Megan made a face before smiling back.

During the journey Luca told Megan his sister, Laura, was looking forward to meeting her and had arranged time off from her work at the museum to prepare lunch for them all. He told her about his freelance work, which involved working with Piccolo Mondo among other publications.

'Are you from Verona?' Megan asked.

'I'm from a small village just outside Verona. My family own an olive farm, which my older brother now manages. However, I do live in Verona with my partner, not too far from Laura.'

'Oh,' Megan said. 'I assumed your friend in the UK was your girlfriend. It's not my business, sorry.'

Luca laughed. 'Julia is a university friend, who offered us the use of her flat while we were visiting the UK.'

'Ah yes.' Megan fiddled with her

sunglasses. Then to fill the silence she continued, 'It would be lovely to meet your partner. I assume you drop in to visit Laura on occasion.'

'On many occasions.' Luca laughed out loud. 'My partner Roberto is never away. He is an artist, and Laura works in the Gallery Museum. They chatter endlessly.' He took one hand off the wheel to imitate chattering mouths.

Megan laughed at his description of them.

'I haven't put you off sharing with my sister?' Luca asked concern in his voice.

'No, not at all, it sounds like fun,' Megan answered, happy that they seemed to be a close family. 'I do have a confession to make, however. That day in the car park you and your brother scared the life out of me, and almost made me change my mind about travelling on my own.'

She stopped speaking as Luca pulled into a parking space on a wide street, where brightly coloured flowers in terracotta pots decorated the balconies of the houses.

Luca switched the engine off and turned to look at her with his soft brown eyes.

'My brother wanted to run after you.' He hesitated. 'I am a photographer, Megan, I see things other people don't notice. I saw fear in your eyes and prevented him from doing so. I was concerned for you, even though I didn't know our paths would again cross after that day. I am so pleased you didn't give in to your fears.'

He reached out and touched her hands, clasped so tightly on her lap the knuckles were blanched white.

'Now let's get inside before Laura rushes out onto the street to ask what's holding us up.'

Surprised by Luca's words and compassion, Megan took a few moments to catch her breath. The short journey from the airport had been incredibly enlightening about the character of her co-worker and she considered herself lucky to be able to share this assignment with him.

Laura, as it turned out, was a younger, more energetic version of Luca and Megan felt herself enveloped in the warmth of her welcome. She felt relieved and safe in this homely flat with a beautiful extended terrace overlooking an area leading to a grassy park with a river running close by and hills fading off into the distance.

'You have a beautiful home, and the view is stunning. Thank you so much for allowing me to live here while I am working in Verona,' Megan said gratefully.

'It belongs to our family, but I have taken it over since my brother Luca moved out. There are four bedrooms, it's really too big for me. Luca keeps a room for storing his work and we have a spare for visitors although Mama and Papa never stay over.' She laughed. 'So, Megan, I shall enjoy having someone to share with me. As you will discover, it is within walking distance to the main attractions and I can walk to work each day,' Laura explained.

As she spoke, she served up lunch.

'I wasn't sure what your taste would be, so I have made a tomato, mozzarella and basil salad with home-made dressing and cold meats with fresh bread. We have sweet pastries to follow with coffee. But I can make something else for you if you would prefer.'

'This is perfect, Laura. It looks delicious, and all so fresh too.' She took out her phone. 'Do you mind if I take a photograph? This is my first meal as I start my adventure. It's for social media.'

'How exciting, Megan! I don't think my cooking has ever had a worldwide audience before. Please feel free.' Laura laughed.

Megan felt slightly embarrassed photographing the table in front of Luca. The vibrant red and white colours of the crockery complemented the food Laura had prepared. She sneaked a sideways glance at him; he was smiling broadly, clearly enjoying her awkwardness.

'Maybe I'll need to take some tips from you,' she joked and they both laughed.

What a wonderful welcome to Verona, a

beautiful fresh salad and sweet treats too. I am going to enjoy my stay. Megan's next social media post winged its way into the world.

She was helping Laura tidy up after lunch and anticipating going to Piccolo Mondo to meet her new colleagues, when she heard the front door open and a man's voice call out to Laura.

'It is Giovanni,' Laura said, moving back into the dining area.

Megan could hear laughter as Laura and Luca greeted their brother good-humouredly. She lingered in the kitchen area, unsure whether to interrupt the greetings.

'Megan, come meet Giovanni!' Laura shouted through to her.

Megan ran her hands over her hair and smoothed down her clothes before venturing into the other room. As she did so, a tall man moved towards her.

'Megan, may I introduce you to Giovanni,' Luca said. 'Our older brother.'

Megan could see the resemblance between the siblings immediately, although Giovanni did not have the care-free look of Luca and Laura. He seemed more serious, almost sombre. This was despite the fact he was dressed in a Lycra cycling outfit in fluorescent colours.

'Good afternoon. I am very pleased to meet you, officially.' Giovanni reached out to greet her and kissed both sides of her face. He was taller than Luca and his hands held her shoulders, causing a rush of heat to flow through her. In contrast to the gorgeous spicy smell of Luca, and the floral scent of Laura, Giovanni had a woodiness about him, a clean musky male smell, which surprised her given that he must have cycled to the flat. She struggled to avert her eyes from his tanned, muscular legs.

'And you,' she answered, unsure about this handsome man in the bright clothes who stood before her. 'Thank you for rescuing my keyring. The photo is very precious to me.'

Giovanni smiled, causing Megan's heart to skip a beat.

'I am very fond of my own dog. Your

dog reminded me of him. Sometimes our pets are easier to understand than people, and often more loyal. I cannot believe our paths crossed again, but I am pleased they have. I am also sorry if we frightened you — it was not our intent.'

His brown eyes softened as he spoke and held her gaze, then abruptly he turned towards Laura.

'I hoped I could use the shower in the guest room. I cycled here from the farm and have a meeting in the city hall.'

'And what would you do if I said no?' Laura laughed. 'Turn up for your licensing meeting dressed like that?' She indicated his cycling gear.

'Actually, I hoped you would be at work and would never know.' Giovanni laughed back at her.

Megan was amazed at the change in Giovanni when he laughed, his face relaxed, his eyes danced with mischief, and his smile lit up the room showing off teeth that glowed white in contrast to his olive coloured skin.

'Well, I guess we had better head to

the office, Megan,' Luca said.

'Give me a moment to freshen up, and I'll be right with you,' Megan answered. Amid the family teasing she had almost forgotten her afternoon appointment. She wanted to change into a blouse, but hoped her well-cut jeans would be acceptable office wear as they were back home.

'I still can't believe you really are going back to work for that magazine,' Giovanni muttered.

'Well, I am,' Luca answered, and Megan saw his jaw tighten.

'Even after the damage they caused to the family?' Giovanni spoke quietly and Megan could feel the tension between the two brothers rise.

'It's my job — it's what I do, Giovanni.' Luca avoided his brother's gaze.

Giovanni's face darkened once more and as he made his way to the guest suite to shower, he said, 'Keeping this family's heritage intact is what I do, Luca. One day you'll realise that.'

★ ★ ★

31

Luca was quiet as he drove them to the office and Megan wondered just how much she should ask following the brothers' conversation. She reasoned that since Luca had been the one to put her in this situation where she was sharing a flat with his sister, then perhaps he owed her a bit of an explanation.

'Your brother Giovanni seems a bit more . . .' She struggled to find the right word. 'He's more serious than you and Laura.'

'And pompous and single-minded and is the only one who gives his life to the family,' Luca answered. With a chuckle he continued, 'And of course, he is right. He does run the family business, growing olives. Our father has gradually handed over to Giovanni in recent years. Laura and I are happy to help when needed, but we have other lives. I love my brother dearly — but olives all day every day, not so much.'

'Why doesn't he want you working with the magazine?' Megan asked.

'Ah, there is a person who works

there — Anna — and she and Giovanni had a disagreement.'

'That doesn't seem a reason to dislike a magazine.'

'Anna wrote an article on the olive farm that was untruthful and caused a loss of business. Claudia did force Anna to write an apology correcting the misinformation, which she published, but some damage was done.' Luca shrugged.

'Anna doesn't sound very responsible,' Megan remarked.

'Well, you will soon find out. You will be working together.' Luca pulled into a space in front of a tall building with a sign that read *Piccolo Mondo Publishing*.

Megan found the magazine office a pleasant oasis of calm. The narrow glass panels placed into the open brickwork made the rooms bright and she imagined would lend a coolness to the rooms in the height of the summer.

Luca knocked on the door of a room situated at the back of the office and opened into another bright, cool room, furnished with metal and glass tables.

Two women were seated at a long table. One rose to greet them.

'Ah, you must be Megan. I am delighted to meet you.' She wore an ivory blouse and a dark pencil skirt which showed off her bronze, tanned legs, and a pair of five-inch heels. Her outfit was simple but gave her an air of classic style, carried off effortlessly. She greeted Megan with a kiss on both cheeks. 'I am Claudia, and I look forward to working with you on our joint assignment.'

'Thank you, Claudia. I am very pleased to be working with you too,' Megan answered.

'And this is Anna.' Claudia waved in the direction of the woman at the table who made no effort to rise to greet Megan. 'Anna will be your point of contact in the office and will be available to assist with whatever needs occur.'

'Thank you. It's nice to meet you, Anna.'

Anna did not offer a reply.

Throughout the rest of the afternoon the group discussed the plan which Bob and Claudia had worked on and agreed or made minor changes as necessary. Towards five o'clock Megan could feel herself flagging despite the copious amounts of coffee provided, and was relieved when Claudia decided they had covered everything and felt confident they all knew their role and deadlines.

Megan waited in the foyer for Luca, feeling optimistic about the assignment and relieved to find Claudia so welcoming and helpful.

She spotted Anna walking towards the exit. Megan moved forward to wish her goodnight, only to be stopped in her tracks by the look of fury on Anna's face.

'Do not think I am going to be your friend, Megan. This should have been my assignment. You with your social media and your little blog, do you really think you are an influencer? Look at you.' She cast her eyes up and down Megan as she spoke. 'I will do as asked by Claudia, but I have no intention of making your life easy.' She spotted Luca in the distance. 'And as for the Rossi family, I'll destroy that jumped-up Giovanni and you with him if need be.' Her eyes flashed with anger as she turned and walked off.

Her venom left Megan trembling. Then she saw Luca looking concerned, and gave herself a shake. This was not the playground, and she was not going to go running to the teacher or her colleagues. Anna would not succeed in intimidating her, but there was no doubt she was dangerous. For now, she needed to reassure Luca that all was well, and hope that Anna's words, spoken in jealousy, were only empty threats.

3

Megan opened her eyes and for a few seconds she couldn't think where she was. The unfamiliar room was light and cool. The walls, painted plain white, were brightened by canvases painted in terracotta, reds and oranges, and Megan felt cosy in her sleepy state.

Her eyes adjusted to the light and she remembered it was her first day of work in Verona, and this was her bedroom in her new home. Megan pulled back the curtains and drank in the magnificent view before her. The sky beyond the hills was tinged yellow, with the first rays of sunlight casting a cheerful glow over the river.

She reached for her mobile phone and snapped the scene, posting it to her social media account with the tagline, *Wow, just wow, what a beautiful view to wake up to this morning. Bring it on, Verona! I'm ready to explore the City of Love.*

She smiled and once more thanked her lucky stars that she had been chosen for this assignment and the luck that led to Luca offering his sister's apartment to share.

The thought of Luca brought her back to reality. She needed to be showered and dressed before he arrived for their first real day working together.

The previous evening, Megan and Laura had come to an arrangement about shopping, cooking and cleaning which suited them both.

When Megan entered the kitchen after having showered and dressed, she was greeted by the delicious aroma of fresh coffee. Laura was in the process of preparing her own packed lunch.

'Good morning, Megan,' Laura greeted her. 'I am late.' She shrugged. 'As usual. There is coffee already made and the fridge is full of cold meats, eggs, fruit, I usually just have some fruit and yogurt for breakfast. You help yourself, I must rush. Oh, we may be going to visit Mama and Papa for dinner. Luca will explain.' With that she grabbed her bag, keys and jacket and was gone.

Megan was left wondering whether 'we' meant Laura and Luca, or was she included? And if so, why — and what should she wear?

She was still agonising over the possible invitation when Luca arrived.

'Ah, you have the coffee pot on. I have brought pastries, and maps for us to plan the day.'

'Thank you, Luca. I haven't managed to make breakfast as yet. I got distracted. The pastries are most welcome.'

'Prego.' Luca gave the polite Italian response. 'Now, I have brought some guides, but you need to find where to collect them so we can add to this collection today.'

'Good, yes, I need to be able to give all that information for the article. Also no car today, Luca, I need to find my way around either by walking or public transport.' Megan poured coffee for them both as she spoke. 'Do you mind if we take this onto the terrace? It's still a novelty to me.'

'Before I forget,' Luca said, 'you have been invited to join us for family dinner at my mama and papa's tonight.'

'Laura mentioned it, but I wasn't sure if I was included in the invite.'

'You are the special guest, Megan.'

'No pressure, then.' She made a face at Luca, who laughed.

'Is that why you were late with breakfast, choosing an outfit to impress Mama and Papa?'

'Of course not,' Megan answered indignantly, then smiled. She loved the easy relationship she and Luca had slipped into. 'And I'm lying, of course — you are correct. I had a slight panic when Laura mentioned it before she left this morning.'

'They are down-to-earth people who will not judge you on your outfit. They just want to know who is sharing the apartment with their daughter.'

'That's a relief. I hadn't thought of it that way. They must be concerned about whether I am a suitable person.'

'You needn't have concerns about impressing them.' Luca lowered his cup as he watched Megan's face. 'Of course, Giovanni, well . . .'

Megan felt herself blush and began clearing away their cups and plates.

'Enough nonsense, let's get on with work.'

Luca laughed with a knowing look. 'If you say so, signorina.'

★ ★ ★

Over the next few hours and with the use of the app on her phone, Megan successfully negotiated her way around many places in Verona that would be helpful to a lone tourist. She found her way to the bus station, the train station and the tourist centre from which she greedily accumulated a mountain of maps and information guides. She checked accommodation in the central area, and places to eat and drink that would be comfortable for someone dining on their own.

Eventually they decided to stop for lunch.

'I think given that we have named the blog From Pizza to Pisa,' Megan said, 'we should really try out some pizza. Where would you recommend?'

'I know a little place. It's off the main tourist route, but worth the walk,' Luca answered.

'Lead the way. Now I have the idea of a pizza in my head, I'm suddenly starving.' Megan laughed.

The tiny restaurant did not disappoint. It was cosy and welcoming, with bright red and white checked tablecloths and walls covered in photos of happy customers. Megan enjoyed the pizza ai funghi, which they decided to share as Luca warned her it would be huge. Megan photographed the monster pizza before posting the photo online with the tagline, *How good does this look?*

Pizza conquered and coffee served, Megan raised the subject of Giovanni and Anna, and why Anna was so angry towards him. She did not share the information that Anna had made it clear her anger now extended to herself.

'I'm not really sure, Giovanni doesn't say too much about it. Whatever happened, the experience shook Giovanni, especially when she caused problems for the farm.'

Megan realised Luca either didn't know what happened or was not prepared to share with her and tactfully she decided to change the subject.

'What would you suggest I take to your parents' home tonight as a gift for inviting me to dinner?'

'That's very kind, but they won't be expecting anything.'

'I know, but my parents instilled good manners into me, as I'm sure yours did in you.' Megan smiled back. 'Flowers, wine, chocolates?'

'My mama loves fresh flowers, so that would be a good choice. I know a nice little florist's shop we can visit on the way home.'

Before they left the restaurant, Megan checked her phone and was astounded to find so many social media messages asking her what type of pizza she'd eaten and how did it rate for taste.

'I can't believe how interested people are in our lunch, but if it helps one visitor to find a nice place to eat then it's worthwhile,' she said.

She took a photo of the menu showing the address and posted it in reply, with the message, *My first pizza during this trip, and the bar has been set high. Absolutely delicious #Yummy*. She turned to Luca. 'I feel a bit self-conscious doing this, I'm not really a hashtag type of person.'

'But you are in Italy now, on an adventure. Maybe you'll discover a new Megan.' He read her comment and added, 'Good idea not to put a rating. That might become complicated, and I still want to be able to eat here when you've gone home.' He laughed.

After a walk around some of the tourist spots they decided to book places on a City Highlights Tour for the following day. Then following a meander

44

through Piazza delle Erbe, with its colourful market stalls they moved up into Via Mazzini. Megan choose some luxury chocolates and true to his word Luca directed her to his favourite flower shop where she purchased gerbera, daisy chrysanthemums and eucalyptus.

Megan's energy was beginning to flag. She was concerned she would fall asleep over dinner.

'Maybe we should consider calling it a day now and head back,' she suggested.

'Good idea, and we could use this as practice for you using the taxi system. Then I will feel confident if you ever need to use one when you're on your own. I can carry on to my apartment after you have been dropped off,' Luca suggested.

Megan agreed this was a useful exercise. She found her way to a taxi rank and was about to enquire how much the fare would be to the apartment, when she stopped short.

'I don't know the address.' She put her hand to her mouth. 'Luca. I have no idea where I'm staying. I think I could walk there — but the number or name of the street is a mystery.'

Luca roared with laughter. 'I suspected as much.' He quickly gave the driver the directions and agreed the charge. Then he joined Megan in the back seat with her shopping.

'I feel such a fool, Luca.' Megan shook her head, but she was also laughing along with Luca.

'An easy mistake. I drove you to the apartment, and all the paperwork was dealt with by your London office. I daresay the need to ask for the address never came up, and I only realised that as we were shopping.'

'And so you decided to test me out.'

'Guilty as charged.'

'Well, thank goodness you did. This will be one of my main pieces of advice on the blog. Always know the address of where you are staying. It will make a good piece, when I explain how I learned that lesson I'm sure it will cause great amusement.'

She rolled her eyes at Luca who drew

his fingers across his lips and twisted them as if turning a lock to indicate he would not disclose her mistake.

★ ★ ★

Laura was already home when Megan arrived back and was in the process of transferring a lemon cake from the shop box into a cake tin. She laughed when she saw Megan watching.

'My mama expects a home-made cake when I visit her. I hate baking and I'm also not particularly good at it, and so I cheat.'

'That's very clever. I must remember to do that when friends visit,' Megan said, placing the flowers and chocolates on the dining table.

'It's not really, my mama is never fooled, but it makes her happy that I go through the process of trying to please her. It's a little thing that makes us smile.' Laura put the lid on the tin. 'I've made a pot of coffee and we have time to relax and enjoy before getting ready for dinner. Luca and Roberto will pick us up en route.'

Megan enjoyed having time to chat and clear her head of all the information swirling around from her day in Verona. She shared with Laura her day's experiences and like her brother Laura laughed as Megan recounted the taxi story.

'I felt so stupid,' Megan said, although she was giggling herself.

It did her good to share a laugh with Laura, whose company she really enjoyed, even though she now knew any chance of keeping her mishap quiet within the Rossi family was probably blown, when this lively girl was in the company of her family this evening.

★   ★   ★

Megan smoothed down the green skater-style dress and checked herself in the mirror. The shade suited her blonde hair and made her blue eyes sparkle. Paired with a pair of brown leather boots and a cream jacket, she felt she achieved a casual but respectful look to meet her friend's parents. As she brushed her lips with a final application of lip gloss, she wondered if Giovanni would be eating with the family.

With a shake of her head, she lifted her shoulder bag and headed out of her room.

'Why ever would you even want to be interested in his plans for the evening?' she said quietly. 'Men bring nothing but trouble.'

'You look lovely, Megan! Those colours really suit you.' Laura admired Megan's outfit. 'If you don't have room in your case for it when you return to the UK, I would be happy to give it a good home.' She laughed.

'You're welcome to borrow it,' Megan replied.

'I was hoping you would say that,' Laura said with a cheeky grin as she threw a denim jacket over her red shirt and skinny navy trousers. 'The boys are here — we'd better get going. Mama's gnocchi will not wait for anyone.'

As it was already dark when they left the city, the journey to the olive farm didn't give Megan much opportunity to observe her surroundings. The conversation between Laura, Luca and Roberto, who was driving, jumped between Italian and English and Megan missed some as they spoke so quickly and like siblings who already know the answers before they ask the questions. She settled back, relaxed and enjoyed their company.

Around thirty minutes later Roberto turned the car into a side road and they drove along a dimly lit track. Megan could just about read a direction sign indicating a turn-off to Rossi's Olive Farm, but they did not follow that road. Instead they turned right and continued until suddenly a brightly lit house and adjacent buildings appeared.

The frontage looked typical farmhouse style to Megan, with bright lanterns giving it a homely welcome glow. The entrance, however, was around the back and it appeared there had been various extensions to increase the original size.

Roberto parked in a courtyard beside a few other vehicles. Megan could now see what appeared to be another house situated across the yard.

The door to the farmhouse was thrown open and two dogs bounded towards them. The larger dog, of indeterminate breed but almost identical to Megan's dog Rufus, headed for Luca. He smiled and said, 'Now you understand why Giovanni knew how precious your keyring was to you. Meet Bobo — he's a bit bouncy but harmless.'

Megan patted the dog who covered her hand in doggy kisses.

'He is adorable, and I can see the likeness.'

'Wait until he eats your best shoes. Not quite so adorable then.' Roberto laughed and ruffled Bobo's fur. 'Are you, boy?'

The other dog, a chihuahua, bounced up into Laura's arms and accepted the hugs and kisses Laura planted on her.

'This is Chichi and she is a little diva,' Luca explained.

A woman, who from her likeness to

Laura Megan assumed to be Mama, stood in the doorway with open arms, eagerly waiting to welcome her children.

4

Megan found herself ushered into the house in a flurry of welcoming embraces and kisses and into a homely kitchen diner, from which the most delicious aroma drifted, making her stomach quietly rumble.

Mama Rossi, who insisted Megan called her Gabriella or Mama, introduced Megan to her husband Marco. He also welcomed her warmly and escorted her towards a chair at the dining table, which was beautifully laid out with an array of brightly coloured crockery and sparking glassware. Marco, Megan noticed, walked with a slight limp as he made his way to the sideboard where a variety of wines were laid out.

'Can I offer you a glass?' He lifted a bottle of red.

'Yes please,' Megan answered, as the others joined her at the table. She felt a pang at the absence of Giovanni, then reasoned perhaps he had something better to do tonight than suffer the company of Laura's flatmate. She smiled at Marco as he poured her a glass of red wine.

From the hall Megan heard voices, an older voice speaking in an Italian dialect Megan could not quite catch or understand, and then in reply, a voice she was sure she did recognise.

'We have a guest for dinner tonight, Nonna, a friend of Luca and Laura's, She's English so you might not understand all she says, but I will sit beside you and translate.'

Some more words Megan could not understand.

'Yes, you have your lacework in your bag, but it's not the time to be repairing nets tonight, we have company.'

This was followed by laughter.

The door opened fully to reveal Giovanni holding the arm of an older lady. He smiled when he saw her, and Megan felt her heart flutter.

'Ah, Megan, good to see you again.' He kissed her cheeks and she once again inhaled the scent of sandalwood from him. 'This is our Nonna, Sylvianna, our papa's mama. She welcomes you to our home.'

Megan was unsure how to greet Nonna and opted for a hug.

'I am honoured to be invited and I'm delighted to share a meal in your home.'

Giovanni translated and Sylvianna smiled.

Gabriella motioned for everyone to be seated. Giovanni helped his grandmother into a seat at the far end of the table, at the opposite end from Megan, and sat beside the older lady.

Megan struggled to keep up with the conversation between the family which took place at speed as everyone caught up with each other's news. As in all families, they also clearly had their own jokes and shorthand for describing events.

The meal was delicious: vegetable soup served with tomato and olive bruschetta, followed by gnocchi, Italian sausage and bean casserole with home-made bread.

Megan found Marco and Giovanni to be very alike in their mannerisms. Marco was polite but reserved. Gabriella, on the other hand, was talkative and keen to know all that was happening with everyone, often all at the same time, which led to multiple conversations taking place.

'Tell me about your family.' Gabriella turned to Megan. 'Do you have brothers and sisters?'

'Yes, I have one of each. I'm the youngest.'

'And what do they do for a living?'

'My brother is a police officer, and my sister is a professional athlete.' She was aware of Giovanni translating to Nonna.

'Is your father a police officer?' Marco asked, surprising Megan at his interest.

'No, my mother and father run a small grocery shop,' Megan answered. 'I'm afraid none of us have followed in their footsteps.'

'Such a shame when that happens in a family. Traditions are lost for ever,' Marco said, playing with the stem of his wine glass.

An uneasy silence fell, broken quickly by the sound of Nonna and Giovanni laughing.

'I am sorry,' Giovanni said. 'I translated to Nonna that your sister makes a living from being an athlete, and Nonna is amazed this is possible. She says she and her friends spent many hours running around the perimeter of the olive grove. She says maybe she could have been an Olympic champion if someone paid her to run.'

The table erupted into laughter and Nonna smiled and raised her glass of wine in response.

'My mother is a character,' Marco said quietly to Megan as the others took up their conversations once more. 'It was a hard life here when she was young, her father farmed the land adjacent to this one and my father and my mother grew up together, both helping out at busy times.

'When they married, the farms over time became one and eventually fell into my father's hands and then into mine. I fear I shall be the last in the line — times change, and like your family we must move on.

'Giovanni is excellent at running the farm; he has a good business head, but he has given up his career to do it, and that is not always for the best. I may not approve of journalists —' he stopped and smiled at her to soften his words and Megan could see Giovanni in his smile. 'But I regret that my eldest son did not follow his chosen career.'

At that point Gabriella cut into their conversation.

'Do you like the apartment, Megan?'

'Yes, very much.' Megan turned her attention away from Marco. 'The views are magnificent.'

'It was my family home,' Gabriella said proudly. 'I inherited it from my parents. They left their food wholesale business to my brothers, and the apartment to me. I think they must have loved me the most.' She laughed a deep, throaty laugh.

To which Marco replied, 'My darling

Gabriella, we all love you the most.' He raised his glass and the family joined in agreement.

Nonna directed a question towards Laura who smiled fondly at her and shook her head. She explained to Megan, 'Nonna is asking if I have a boyfriend.'

'What about the professor?' Luca asked, laughing as he spoke.

'The professor is totally immersed in Dante, I cannot compete. All I ever hear about is Dante and *The Divine Comedy*. I mean, what is wrong with the man?'

Megan was lost until Laura explained, 'Luca is referring to one of my colleagues who is a history professor. He is young and extremely handsome. He also lectures in *The Divine Comedy* and is totally unaware of my existence. His loss, I might add.' She tossed her thick black hair across her shoulders.

'Dante is an important figure in literature,' Giovanni said.

'I think we will see Dante's statue tomorrow on our city tour, aren't we, Luca?' Megan said.

'We are indeed,' Luca answered. 'If we see your professor, would you like us to point out the error of his ways to him, Laura?'

Laura snorted back at her brother.

'I have never read *The Divine Comedy*,' Megan offered. 'Perhaps I should get a copy!'

'Only if you want to be bored for the rest of your stay,' Laura returned, rolling her eyes.

'It is part of our study in Italy, and some of us are more impressed by it than others.' Giovanni nudged his sister's shoulder.

'A bit like Shakespeare, then.'

'Exactly.' Giovanni smiled straight at her making her blush.

'Right, everyone, I'll serve coffee and some of Laura's delicious cake,' Gabriella said, once the dishes had been cleared and the dogs were allowed back into the kitchen. A collective 'Oh, no,' filled the air followed by shouts of 'not for me, no thank you.'

'You are all comics.' Laura stood up.

'It's from a shop, as you know very well. Mama, sit down, I'll serve and make sure they eat every bit.'

'Thank you for a lovely meal, Signora Rossi . . . Gabriella, Mama,' Megan said, flustered. 'It was delicious, and I am absolutely full. Laura, I really cannot eat another bite.'

'All the more for me.' Luca held out his plate.

'And me.' Roberto, held out his plate too.

'You boys are always hungry,' Laura said. 'Giovanni, what about you?'

'Not for me thank you — like Megan, I'm full.'

Megan noticed Nonna had moved to a comfier chair and had pulled out the piece of lace she was working on and set to work, chattering to Gabriella as her fingers moved quickly.

'That is very beautiful, and I can't believe how quickly your fingers are moving, Nonna,' she said. She did not feel comfortable calling this older woman by her first name; it seemed disrespectful.

Then, fearing 'Nonna' was perhaps even more so, she added, 'Signora Rossi, I mean.'

Nonna looked at Megan and smiled as Giovanni explained Megan's words to her. She beckoned for Megan to move towards her and when she did, she kissed her on both cheeks, and indicating herself she said, 'Nonna.' She spoke to Giovanni again, waving her hands.

Giovanni explained, 'My grandmother is carrying out an old tradition. These are nets for the olive trees to protect them from wind and rain, and the birds and insects. She is pleased you find them beautiful. She also wishes for you to call her Nonna.' He smiled as he said, 'She must like you very much.'

'Please tell her I am very honoured.' Megan bent down and kissed the older woman. 'Grazie mille. Thank you very much.'

'She also says I must take you to see the groves. It's dark, although we do have security lighting, so you don't need to if you don't feel like walking around a farm in the dark.'

Giovanni didn't look at Megan as he spoke.

'Of course, I would like to see around the farm. If that's OK, and the rest of the family have no objection?'

'Nonna has asked I show Megan around the farm. Is that OK with everyone? We'll be back before you have finished your cake and coffee.'

'Fine by me,' Luca and Laura said in unison. Chichi attached herself to Laura's side once more.

'I'll keep Nonna company until you get back,' Roberto said, taking a seat beside the older woman who patted his hand and fell into conversation with him.

Gabriella found a warm coat for Megan to put around her shoulders.

'In case you catch a chill,' she said, smiling.

Only Marco seemed concerned.

'Be careful,' he said. Megan was unsure if the warning was to herself or Giovanni.

* * *

The cool night air caught Megan's breath and she was glad of the coat. She noticed Giovanni had lifted a sweater and was pulling it over his head as they moved into the courtyard, Bobo trotting dutifully after him.

'Are you sure you want to do this now?' he asked.

'Yes — although I do hope I can make sense of it in the dark. It will help me walk off dinner, as delicious as it was.'

'Actually, we have a barn that I've converted into an operations room with overhead photos so you can get an idea rather than have to walk too far. Nonna wants you to see the finished nets and I have a collection of them.' Giovanni guided her along a path in front of the other farmhouse she had first spotted when they parked.

He explained, 'This one is where I live.'

'Oh, I assumed you lived in the main house.'

'I can see why. The house has grown over the generations and has a little annexe now too. I prefer to have a little bit of distance at the end of the day and so I choose to live in the other house,' Giovanni explained.

'It's so peaceful here,' Megan murmured, aware of the silence save for a few animal tweets and snuffles and the occasional warning growl from Bobo towards whatever small creatures he could hear or smell. 'And look at the sky — it's like a velvet cushion, with little chinks of diamonds twinkling.' She laughed. 'I'm sorry, I'm getting carried away, you must think I'm mad. I'm just not used to seeing such a beautifully clear sky.'

'That's OK. I like to think it's quite a special place. Wait until you see it in the summer.'

Giovanni stopped at the front of a big barn and opened the lock.

'If you would care to enter, I can fast forward to summer for you now.'

He slipped open a door and from a control panel, lit up the interior of the barn.

Megan was astounded. She expected a dirty old shed, faintly smelling of damp and strewn with long abandoned sacks and other farmyard rubbish. To her amazement this was an ultra-modern office suite. The walls were wood-clad and illuminated by sunken lighting, on which hung various aerial photographs of olive trees, orange trees, kiwi fruit trees and huge orchards. There were tables laid out with models of buildings and various types of machinery. An open staircase led up to another level laid out as an office with computer equipment and angled drawing desks.

Downstairs, one corner of the barn was furnished with an old-fashioned writing desk and shelves of leather-bound books with a cosy sofa in autumnal colours with deep-filled cushions. To the side of the desk lay some wicker baskets with an array of handcrafted throws and, as Megan now recognised, Nonna's olive nets.

'Giovanni, I am lost for words. I never expected this, it's beautiful.' Megan stood struggling to absorb it all, it was so unexpected. As she moved through the barn, she learned the history of the farm and could see the progress through the years and through the seasons.

'Giovanni, this is a beautiful monument to your family's history. You must be very proud.'

From the way he held himself Megan could see he was pleased she recognised the purpose of the barn.

'Thank you. I have tried to merge the old with the new. I just fear it will all be lost and forgotten one day. I suppose this barn keeps me grounded.'

Megan could see how important this was to Giovanni and she chose her words carefully.

'It is all any of us can do, Giovanni — pay homage to the past but look to the future at the same time.'

'Yes, exactly.' He moved towards the bookshelves as he spoke and stroked his hand across the volumes. 'Ah, here it is.' He handed her the book he had removed from its place. 'Dante's *Divine Comedy*.

It's my copy from university. Would you like to borrow it while you are staying here?'

'Oh, I couldn't possibly. What if I lost it?' Megan began to say. 'Or dropped it in the bath . . .' She willed herself to stop talking as she blushed.

Giovanni stifled a chuckle.

'Well, fortunately it's not a new book or especially valuable. It has survived student accommodation and I'm sure all will be OK. I assume you are comfortable reading in Italian, and I can help translate if you find it hard going.' He held the book out to her.

'Thank you, Giovanni. I shall take exceptionally good care of it, I promise.' She smiled up at him.

'I know you will.'

'What did you study at university?' Megan asked, expecting the answer to be business or agriculture.

'Literature.' Megan saw a cloud pass over his face. 'Which is very handy for this line of work.' He threw his hands out to encompass the barn and laughed. The cloud had lifted. 'Now we had better get back — the others will be desperate to return to the big city.'

When they re-entered the big house, the others were in no hurry to leave. Luca and Laura were still lounging on the sofas, and Roberto was helping Nonna to wind up threads.

'You are all so lucky to live in such a beautiful place,' Megan said sincerely. 'And Nonna, your nets are exquisite.'

'I see your walk with Giovanni was worthwhile.' Laura said, pointing towards the book.

'Yes, very.' Megan lowered her head to hide the flush growing up her neck and cheeks as she placed the book in her bag.

'Nonna has a request, Megan,' Roberto said.

'Yes, of course. What can I do, Nonna?' Megan smiled towards her.

'Accompany Giovanni to the Olive Farmers' Ball.' Roberto made a face as he answered. 'Sorry to drop you in it, guys.'

'Nonna!' the room exclaimed.

'I am sorry, Megan,' Marco said. 'My mother can be mischievous at times.'

Nonna meantime chattered to Giovanni and from her hand movements it was clear she was urging her reluctant grandson to say something.

'I have a busy schedule while I am here. I don't think I would be free. Isn't that right, Luca?' Megan looked to Luca to help her out of this embarrassing situation.

'That's true. Megan is very busy,' Luca agreed.

Megan sighed with relief.

Luca went on, 'Unless the ball is this weekend it's probably not convenient. When is it?'

'Saturday night,' Roberto answered, looking daggers at his partner.

'I don't think it's suitable for Megan to attend the dance,' Marco said sombrely. 'After all, she's a journalist — and look what happened the last time one of them attended as our guest.'

Megan wished the ground would open and swallow her. Giovanni broke the silence.

'That is unfair, Papa. Megan is not Anna. Now, Megan, I don't wish to put you on the spot, but it seems we are already there thanks to Nonna.' He smiled at the older lady, and made a face at his brother. 'And feel free to refuse, with no hard feelings, but would you do me the honour of accompanying me to the Olive Farmers and Traders Annual Ball on Saturday night with Luca and Roberto and Laura — and her professor, if she can persuade him to come?'

Giovani's siblings groaned that they were now involved. Gabriella and Marco roared with laughter, lightening the atmosphere once more.

'How can I refuse such an offer? It will be my pleasure, Giovanni. Thank you for asking.'

It was soon time to leave and Luca, Roberto and Laura joked they were leaving Megan behind as punishment for their being invited to the ball.

'You can't leave me — I don't know my address.' Megan laughed, then had to explain to the others about the incident with the taxi. It made her happy to have shared the evening with these lovely people. She hoped the remainder of her trip would be just as warm and welcoming.

Nonna sat smiling in the corner, content that her request had been fulfilled.

* * *

As Megan lay in bed that night, having emailed her notes from the day to Tracey and written some words for her blog, she felt thankful to have met Luca and his lovely family. Although she missed her own family, the Rossi family had immediately welcomed her into theirs. It made being away from home and in another country less overwhelming.

She gazed at a photograph of the night sky she had taken at the farm.

How can this night sky not delight and enchant? There's magic in that velvet pillow dusted with stars. She hit the Post button sending it out, and fell into a deep and peaceful sleep.

5

Next morning as arranged Megan set off to meet Luca. Walking through the city, she felt a sense of achievement that she could already find her way around.

She smiled, remembering the text she had woken up to from her sister Chloe.

I've just read your post from last night and I want to know all the details about whoever you were sharing that star-filled night with. And don't try to fool me, I'm your big sis. Love and miss you, speak soon xx

It brought a spring to Megan's step just thinking about describing the previous evening to her sister.

'Ciao, Megan, how are you? I was worried you would have been on the first flight home, after meeting the family. They can be a bit full-on, as you found out. I'm so sorry about the whole annual ball thing. Please feel free to change your mind — I won't hold it against you.'

Luca gave her a lopsided grin as he

kissed her cheek.

'Good morning, Luca. I am very well, and I had a lovely time last night.' She smiled at him. 'I didn't realise how I would miss my own family and last night made me feel part of yours, even for just a short time. And as for not going to the dance, well I'm not about to back down. I wouldn't like to see Nonna when she's angry.'

Luca laughed out loud. 'I think you are a very, wise woman Megan. Come on — let's get on with our tour. There is a lot to cover.'

Megan soon discovered Luca was not exaggerating when he explained how much there was to explore in the UNESCO-protected city.

She loved L'Arena from the velvet curtains at the entrance, to sitting on the stone steps imagining all the events that had taken place there in the past.

They moved on to Piazza Dante where Megan marvelled at the statue of the great author and smiled at the memory of the evening before.

'Hey, what are you smiling at?' Luca shouted towards her as she posed at the statue.

'Nothing.'

'Nothing? I think it might be a certain book loaned to you by a certain someone, written by a certain author looking down on you right now.'

'Are you certain?' She laughed back at him.

'Time for Casa di Giulietta, I think.' Luca arched his eyebrows at her.

'I'm not sure that's an attraction a lone traveller would visit. Do you? Would you?' Megan asked.

'It's on the list,' Luca said. 'And it's something you can even advise people to avoid if you think that's for the best.'

As it turned out, Megan enjoyed seeing Juliet's balcony. The industry that had grown up around it amused her, from notepaper to cushions, keyrings, mugs, everything covered in love hearts, like a perpetual Valentine's Day.

They next climbed Torre Dei Lamberti and were rewarded with a panoramic view of the city which took her breath away. They then explored the Galleria d'Arte Moderna where Laura worked and were delighted to be introduced to her colleague, the professor, who was indeed young and handsome and called Bruno.

'Laura tells me you are interested in Dante.' He shook her hand enthusiastically.

'Well I'm not sure just yet. I've still to read . . .'

Laura interrupted.

'Bruno, Megan and Luca are waiting to eat lunch.'

'Ah, of course. I shall see you both again on Saturday night. Laura has very kindly invited me to the event — perhaps we shall have an opportunity to discuss Dante during the evening.' Bruno made his way back to his office situated in the adjacent Torre Dei Lamberti.

Laura rolled her eyes at Megan.

'Now do you see my problem? Always Dante, never Laura.'

'Maybe he needs to visit Casa di

Giulietta for some inspiration,' Megan suggested. Laura laughed as she took her arm and led her towards the nearby restaurant.

'I shall leave you ladies to enjoy your lunch,' Luca said. 'I have another job I need to finish. Would you like me to meet you later to go home?'

'No, thank you, Luca. I'm going to check in with Claudia in the office before I head back.'

'OK — we'll speak later then, ciao.' He kissed them both lightly on the cheek and headed out.

Megan followed Laura's lead and ordered a light salad with pomegranate and pine nuts.

'My waistline can't afford to keep eating huge meals every day of the week.'

'Mama does go overboard with the portions, but you need to keep your energy up after all that walking. Now what are you going to wear to this ball we have all been tricked into attending?'

'I have absolutely no idea. I didn't pack a ball gown in my suitcase. I'll have a wander through the shops on my way back — maybe I'll be able to pick up a sale bargain. What about you, do you have something picked out?'

'Megan, I am going with Bruno; I could turn up wearing one of Nonna's olive nets and he would say Dante used to wear one in a similar style.'

They both laughed out loud, causing other people around them to turn and stare. Through the giggles Laura managed to speak.

'I have a gown I've been desperate to wear. I just wish it was to a more exciting event.'

As Megan made her way to the office, she wondered what she could possibly find to wear within her budget that would be suitable for a formal event. She also wondered if she should mention the event to Claudia. She was, after all, attending in her own time and at her own expense, but Megan was afraid there could have been a conflict due to Anna's previous article involving Giovanni and his family. She decided she would rather mention it to Claudia than have her find out from someone else.

She was pleased she had phoned ahead to ensure Claudia would be available to see her, especially when she saw Anna.

'Why are you here? There is no need for you to disturb Claudia. Just leave whatever you want her to check or sign off and I'll get it done,' Anna greeted her, accompanied by a dismissive flourish of her hand towards her desk, which Megan took to mean she was to drop her paperwork, assuming she had any, on Anna's desk.

Megan painted a smile on her face.

'Good afternoon Anna, how are you? I hope you are well. Thank you for the offer, but I have already arranged to meet with Claudia.'

As she spoke Megan made her way towards Claudia's office, pleasantly greeting other staff members. By the time she reached the door, her legs were shaking from her attempt at a display of confidence.

As Megan entered the room, Claudia rose from behind her desk, dressed in a fitted red dress and short white jacket the image of elegance, and came forward to greet her.

'Ah, Megan, how lovely to see you.'

Megan suddenly became aware of her own outfit — khaki cargo pants, a white T-shirt and loose-fitting khaki V-necked jumper.

'I have been reading some of your draft articles. You have already been busy, and I am impressed with your work. I like your style of writing,' Claudia continued.

'Thank you,' Megan answered. 'That was one of the reasons I wanted to meet with you today, just to make sure I am on the right track for your magazine. I was aware my magazine in the UK and yours here in Italy are looking for the same articles but from different angles. I'm pleased if you are happy with what I've written so far.'

'The social media was a brilliant idea. Bob tells me it was your suggestion. I believe our Twitter account has been bombarded with restaurants asking you to try their pizza and readers offering recommendations. I'll get a list drawn up and you could perhaps get around as many as you feel you can just to keep our readers happy.'

'I'll be happy to try, providing my trouser size doesn't expand too much.' Megan heaved a sigh and Claudia smiled.

'And what was the other reason for your visit?' Claudia held Megan's gaze.

'Pardon?' Megan was confused.

'You said the article was one reason, therefore there must have been another.'

'Ah yes, well, you see...'

'Just rip the plaster off Megan.' Claudia encouraged.

'I've been invited, and I still don't really know how or why, to the olive farmers' ball, and I wanted to be sure you have no objection to me going.' There was now a trickle of sweat running down Megan's back. Why did Claudia make her feel as though she was in front of the head teacher?

'Are you looking at this as part of

the assignment, or representing the company?'

'No, I was invited by Giovanni Rossi and his family.'

'Ah, the handsome Giovanni.' Claudia raised her eyebrows. 'I can see why you might feel there is a conflict. Anna accompanied him one year and then wrote a scathing article, which transpired to be untrue, for which she was lucky to keep her job. I have no objection, Megan, but I must warn you, we — that is the magazine — shall be covering the event and Anna will be in attendance along with our sub-editor Eduardo. I would not want there to be any trouble on the night.'

'There will not be any trouble from me, Claudia, I can assure you,' Megan answered, her heart lighter now that she had Claudia's approval to attend. She stood up to leave.

'Just one more thing,' Claudia said. 'What do you intend to wear?' Her eyes ran up and down Megan as she spoke.

Megan shuffled uncomfortably.

'I'm not really sure. I'm going to have a quick look in the stores on the way home.'

Claudia moved towards her desk and opening a drawer, leafed amongst a few business cards.

'Here.' She handed Megan a card. 'This is my friend's business and she is due me a favour. I'll give her a call and she'll fit you out with the loan of everything you need. Would that be helpful?'

'Oh, Claudia! That would be wonderful. I don't want to let the family down — they have been very welcoming towards me. Thank you so much.'

'You are very welcome Megan.' Claudia smiled warmly. 'And Giovanni will be a very lucky man to have you on his arm.'

★   ★   ★

The day of the olive farmer's ball found the apartment in a swirl of preparations. After visiting a hairdresser, beautician and nail technician, Megan felt exhausted before the evening even began. It didn't help when Laura announced that Giovanni would be staying over in the guest bedroom after the ball, sending Megan into a frenzy of cleaning and clearing away any scrap of her existence in the apartment, for fear he thought her an untidy slob.

Laura shook her head at her.

'You worry too much about other people's opinions. Relax! Stop judging yourself so harshly.'

Taking the opportunity to put her feet up for half an hour, Megan smiled to herself that for two people who were reluctant guests at the upcoming ball, she and Laura had certainly put in an amazing amount of effort to look their best.

Her borrowed dress in its cover hung from the wardrobe door and she relived the thrill of excitement when she arrived at Claudia's friend's shop and saw the beautiful array of garments.

The woman, introducing herself as

Rosario, explained she stocked a mix of previously owned designer dresses and new ones by emerging designers. She picked out a few to suit Megan's shape and colouring and Megan spent the rest of the afternoon trying them on, amazed to even find herself in this situation. Eventually she settled on a strapless ballerina-length emerald green creation with a layer of taffeta beneath the skirt and a bodice embroidered with green, blue and gold threads. Rosario found matching accessories in gold and green and even some costume jewellery to complete the outfit.

Megan could not thank her enough and promised she would take good care of it all.

Rosario joked, 'My friend Claudia says she will take it out of your salary if anything happens.'

'I'm not sure how many years' salary that would take,' Megan answered, feeling slightly unsure about accepting the offer.

'We are just joking with you, my dear,'

Rosario said. 'Claudia is a good friend to me, and I trust her judgement. You wear this outfit and do not worry. I hope you have the most wonderful evening.' She kissed her on both cheeks.

When Megan saw Laura in her red, full-length sheath dress, a geometric bow covering one shoulder leaving the other bare, she gasped.

'Laura, you are absolutely stunning. Bruno will have his work cut out tonight keeping admirers at bay.' She moved to see the dress from all angles. 'Here, let me take a photo of you and I'll send it to your mobile, for Mama and Papa to see.'

'Thank you, but I won't send it to them tonight, or Papa will turn up at the ball with his don't-go-near-my-daughter face.' She giggled. 'Let me do the same for you, Megan. You look gorgeous. I am not even going to walk beside you tonight, I don't want the competition.'

Laura pouted, then laughed.

'You chose well. The dress, and you, are beautiful; the cut and colour suit your figure. I'm sure there will be many men tonight whose jaws will drop when you walk into the room.'

Megan shook off Laura's compliments. Compared to Laura, she knew she came a poor second. She loved the dress and looked her best, but she had never been a natural beauty, unlike Laura. She sent the photo to her mother and sister; they would be pleased to see her getting out and making friends.

Bruno had agreed to pick up the girls and they would meet the others at the venue, a few kilometres outside the city. As the venue came into sight via a tree-lined avenue, Megan exclaimed at its splendour. It was in typical baroque style and set in manicured gardens. Lit by torchlight, it enticed them into its walls.

The girls and Bruno, in his black tie dinner suit, made their way into the marble foyer sumptuously decorated in rich velvets. They were met by Luca and Roberto, looking very handsome in their tuxedos. Luca had opted for silver and Roberto for burgundy, and they complemented each other perfectly. Across the room Megan spotted Anna dressed in a long white sheath dress with a slit from ankle to thigh, amongst a group of men. Megan noted the sub-editor was not among them.

After a few moments chatting, the guests heard the bell ring indicating it was time for them to enter the ballroom for dinner and the group made their way into the room. Megan felt disappointed Giovanni hadn't yet arrived.

Her attention as she descended the flight of marble stairs was momentarily distracted by the splendour of the ballroom glistening with gold and crystal decorations, and lit by magnificent Murano glass chandeliers, that at first she didn't see Giovanni at the foot of the stairs, his eyes upon her as she descended towards him. He stepped forward and welcomed her with a kiss on the cheek, and offered his arm to escort her to the table. Megan's heart skipped a beat to be on the arm of this tall, dark, handsome man, who really did look like James Bond in his tuxedo.

Giovanni bent down and whispered. 'You look beautiful, Megan, absolutely stunning.'

Megan could barely whisper back, 'Thank you, Giovanni, you are truly kind. And you too are very handsome tonight.'

Out of the corner of her eye, she saw Anna watching them and a shiver ran down her spine.

It transpired the event was more fun than any of them expected. Giovanni was presented with an award for Best Flavoured Oil from an Established Tree, and his siblings were amazed he had kept the nomination a secret.

He just shrugged. 'I didn't expect to win.'

After the award ceremony, Anna appeared at the table to congratulate Giovanni, carrying a glass of red wine. Reaching forward to kiss him, she tilted her glass towards Megan who froze as the contents began to spill in her direction.

A vision of Claudia and Rosario's faces

appeared before her as she prepared for the shock of the wine hitting her dress, when suddenly Giovanni stepped back from Anna. In doing so, his hand moved upwards, connecting with the glass and making it change direction. The wine flew from the glass and with a flourish splattered over Anna. The red liquid bled into the white sheath dress in an ever-expanding stain.

There was a collective intake of breath from those seated around the table, broken by the sound of Anna screeching.

'You did that on purpose. I came to congratulate you, and this is what you do.'

To everyone's surprise, Bruno spoke.

'If I might say,' he began, 'what happened was nothing more than an accident. You were aiming the glass towards my friend here.' He pointed towards Megan. 'And the corrective measure put in place by my other friend —' this time he pointed towards Giovanni — 'caused the forward motion of the wine to change direction but with increased velocity, thus resulting in the offending liquid escaping in the direction of yourself.' He nodded towards Anna. 'An unfortunate event, the principal cause being the angle you were holding your glass at when you approached my friends.'

Someone shouted, 'Well done, young man! A superb explanation.'

A member of staff approached the table to offer assistance, but not before Eduardo appeared at Anna's side.

'I am sorry.' He spoke to Giovanni. 'For my colleague's outburst — caused by shock, I think.'

'Do not apologise on my behalf!' Anna hissed.

'Then I suggest you do so yourself. No? Then my next suggestion is for you to step into the car I have just ordered for you.'

'I'm going. I only tried to be civil, but I should have known better.'

Megan saw Giovanni's jaw tighten but he remained silent as Anna turned and walked away, her head high and her eyes daring anyone to comment directly towards her.

'Well, that was a performance.' Luca broke the silence.

'She's always unhappy about something,' Laura said. 'But you, my little warrior, you were fantastic.' Laura kissed Bruno on the cheek, and he blushed profusely and allowed her to lead him on to the dance floor.

Megan realised the evening could descend into melancholy, or they could brush themselves off and move on. She took a deep breath.

'I don't know about you guys, but Nonna wanted us to enjoy this event and I intend to carry out her wishes. So which one of you gentlemen would like to ask me to dance?'

She threw the challenge down praying she wouldn't be left looking like a fool.

To her surprise, it was Giovanni who stood up.

'Would you care to join me on the dance floor, Megan?'

'I believe I would, thank you.' Megan smiled and took the hand he offered, enjoying the feeling of her hand in his.

Luca and Roberto whooped as Giovanni and Megan made their way on to the floor. Megan giggled and waved to encourage them to join the dancers, which they happily did.

The evening which could have been a disaster became a good night. They all danced until Megan wondered if her poor feet would ever recover.

On the journey home, with Bruno the designated driver, Laura in the front seat and Megan and Giovanni in the back, Megan listened as Laura and Bruno chattered non-stop.

She had enjoyed the closeness of Giovanni on the dance floor and felt slightly apprehensive at the thought of him staying overnight in the apartment, but she wondered what this man next to her was thinking. As if to answer her unspoken question, she felt his hand reach out in the darkness and gently wrap around hers.

6

Not for the first time during the journey, Megan wondered what on earth she was doing on a coach surrounded by German tourists and heading up narrow roads, with drops she couldn't even bear to think about, towards the snow-covered Dolomites.

This was her first big adventure on her own, as part of her assignment. This trip was arranged by Piccolo Mondo, or more specifically by Anna and involved Megan's participation in the activities provided in the area, mostly winter sports, with the group of tourists who comprised adult single travellers of various ages. The higher the coach climbed, the more concerned Megan became for her lack of skiing experience.

Thankfully, she had the luxury of a double seat to herself which removed the need to try to make small talk, and so she used the time to check up on social media and messages from her family. Following the Olive Farmer's Ball, and subsequent hushed phone calls with her sister, Megan now found herself bombarded with messages from Chloe demanding updates on the 'dishy farmer' as she called him, and was not put off with Megan's disappointingly truthful answers of 'there is nothing to tell'.

She thought back to the evening of the ball, when Giovanni held her hand and something she could not describe passed between them. Now she wondered if it was just her imagination; maybe the wine and the headiness of a lovely evening. When they arrived home from the ball Laura kissed Bruno and sent him on his way. Megan became self-conscious and very much aware of Giovanni's presence.

Laura made hot chocolate for herself and Megan but Giovanni excused himself, said goodnight and made his way to the guest room. Laura, exhausted from dancing, also said goodnight and took her drink to own room, leaving Megan alone with a mug of hot chocolate and her thoughts.

She stared in the direction of the guest suite, before she reluctantly took herself off to bed and tried hard to forget the presence of the man in the room next to hers.

When she awoke in the morning it was to discover Giovanni already gone.

* * *

With a jolt Megan became aware of her surroundings and looked around the coach furtively, praying she hadn't actually dozed off. She could now see the ski lifts snaking up the mountains, and when she dared to look further out the window, tiny groups of wooden houses and brightly coloured buildings lay scattered among the snow-covered slopes. She moved closer to the window to appreciate the views which were like a picture-perfect postcard. Now she could appreciate the magnificence of the mountains which despite the significant height the coach had already climbed, still towered over them.

Megan was thankful when the driver turned off the main road, drove through the village resort and towards the hotel where they would be staying during the trip.

From the animated conversations, some of her fellow passengers seemed to have either already made friends or know each other from previous tours and made a note to ask them at some point during the week about their circumstances.

She smiled and chatted with some of the others as they waited to collect their luggage, pleased to be able to stretch her legs. Eventually they piled into the hotel. Megan held back, aware this was a working trip for her and not a holiday. She allowed the others to check in first, giving her an opportunity to take photos of the resort.

She snapped the view of the mountains and sent it to her social media accounts with the tagline, *Did someone say the only way is up? Gulp . . . seems quite a climb to me!* Before she managed to return her phone to her pocket, she could hear some pings indicating the message had been read and liked or responded to or both. She smiled at the speed of the response to her post, good or bad. She was still smiling as she approached the reception desk. The receptionist, a tall, dark-haired girl, addressed her in German, as she had done with the other guests, but then realised Megan was more comfortable speaking in Italian.

Megan gave her name and the girl checked her computer, then asked Megan for her passport. After several attempts it became clear there was no room booked for Megan, and neither Anna nor Claudia were available in the office.

Megan drew a deep breath, as she remembered this was just the situation Bob had given her the travel card for.

'I can only assume a mistake has happened somewhere with the office; however, I would be grateful if I could make a reservation for this week using this card.'

'I am sorry, Miss Hopkins, we have no free rooms available his week,' the girl answered.

Megan felt her stomach tighten. 'Thank you. Perhaps you could recommend another hotel?'

'I shall try for you, but I have to advise there is a snowboard competition taking place this week and the hotels are very busy.'

Megan thanked her and it took a minute for her to realise her predicament. She was stranded on her own in a strange country. Suddenly the perils of being a lone traveller struck home.

After what seemed an eternity the receptionist informed Megan all the hotels in the resort were full and directed her to the nearby information centre. 'Perhaps they have details of B&Bs which may suit your requirements.'

Megan had no choice but to take her advice and trundle her luggage towards the information centre which she prayed was open. She tried to keep calm by telling herself she would be visiting the information centre as part of her research at some point during her trip; this was just killing two birds with one stone. She gazed upwards towards the snow-covered mountains, which to an anxious Megan, now took on a menacing air.

When she reached the centre, it was to discover it was already full of skiers all looking for places to stay or trying to book on the best slopes.

As she waited, she filled her bag with numerous leaflets to use in her articles including one advertising car hire and decided if all else failed, hiring a car to return to Verona would be her last option. As nervous as she already felt, the idea of driving down the roads the coach had just climbed filled her with a new level of fear.

Eventually it was her turn in the queue, and the pleasant assistant listened to her predicament and checked his computer.

'The resort is very busy this week as you already know.' He tapped on his keyboard as he spoke. 'Ah, I may have something for you.'

Megan felt her heart leap.

'Now it is a small bed and breakfast provision, which is family run. It is a few miles out and you would need to take a taxi journey to get there, but I can arrange that for you, or there is a shuttle bus. Would that be suitable?' he asked.

Megan could have cried with relief.

'Yes, oh yes — that would be very suitable.'

The taxi drive to the B&B allowed Megan to view the busy resort with its collection of shops, restaurants, bars, hotels and quaint chalet-style houses. It was bigger than she had anticipated and she was pleased she had made the decision to use the taxi service, although she now had a timetable for the shuttle service, which she would need to use regularly to meet up with the coach party to join their excursions.

Learning from her previous experience, she made sure she placed the address of her new lodgings in a safe place and tried to text the details to Tracey in the London office to also ask her to explain to Bob the reason for the card bill. However the message didn't send as her mobile now did not have a signal.

When the driver pulled alongside the B&B Megan was surprised to find it was bigger than she expected and looked warm and welcoming. Once inside, she found herself almost smothered in friendly greetings from a large woman named Clara who was the owner. She fussed over Megan, offered hot chocolate and showed her into a warm lounge while staff put the finishing touches to her room.

After the cool reception at the hotel, Megan was deeply grateful. She flopped into a cosy sofa beside a log fire which glowed gently giving out a gentle warmth and throwing light onto the exposed beams and into the rustic style lounge.

Just as her eyes began to feel heavy and she felt herself begin to drift off to sleep, Clara bustled in, informing her the room was now ready. She gave Megan a leaflet with details of breakfast times and information on the best bars and restaurants to eat at, and a key for the outside door.

'I hope you enjoy your stay with us.' She smiled warmly. 'We do have a small bar, which we open in the evenings for our guests if you care to join the other guests for a nightcap before bed.'

'Thank you so much. It would be lovely to join the others for a drink tonight,' Megan answered.

Her room surpassed her expectations. She had imagined a tiny cupboard-sized room with a fold-up bed but this room was large, with a double bed covered with a fluffed-up quilt and pillows and cushions in warm reds and greens. A fitted wardrobe with wooden sliding doors took up half of the wall, with an unexpected ensuite bathroom taking up the other half. A wooden dressing table with a bucket chair was opposite wall and to her surprise, a coffee machine sat on a little table.

Megan decided the mix-up over the

hotel booking was ultimately beneficial. A cosy, welcoming B&B such as this would be an ideal base for a lone traveller.

The signal on her mobile was still intermittent. As she had no booking at the hotel and so no meal provision there, she decided to find somewhere local to eat before night fell. Tomorrow she would take the shuttle bus to the hotel to meet up with the group.

A walk along the village street soon revealed an array of delightful little gift and craft shops which were fairly busy. She read the menu outside a few restaurants while trying to peek inside at the seating arrangements. She didn't want to find herself alone at a table designed to seat twelve.

She found the designated stop for the shuttle bus and checked the timetable against the one from the information office, pleased to find they matched. Passing a side street, she noticed a little row of cafes, bakeries and confectioners. The sweet smells made her stomach rumble, reminding her she hadn't eaten since leaving Laura's apartment in the early hours of the morning.

She found a little café with tables set for two and four diners, even more pleased to spy an empty table. A charming waiter happily showed her to the table and left her with a menu while he fetched her a soft drink.

She tried her mobile again, firstly to check if the signal had improved and secondly to give her something to do as she sat alone. Messages popped up from Tracey, Claudia, Chloe, Bob, Luca and — astonishingly — Giovanni.

It seemed that, according to Claudia, Anna mistakenly made the reservation in her own name. Tracey left her a message saying that when Bob discovered Megan had been left stranded, he contacted Claudia and tore her off a strip. Bob left a message apologising and reassuring her the use of the card was fine, congratulating her on her initiative and reminding her to stay safe and to stay in whichever accommodation made her feel more comfortable.

Luca messaged to say he would drive up to collect her if she wanted to return. Giovanni had also offered to collect her, and gave an address and phone number of friends he knew in the area, saying she was to go there if she needed help. He finished by asking her to please call him when she got his message.

Chloe's text was the usual, *How are things? Where are you today? Have you met a handsome ski instructor yet?* And Megan laughed out loud, drawing attention from her fellow diners. Her sister had no idea of the events of Megan's day.

She responded to all the messages as best she could except for Giovanni. She couldn't exactly phone him in the middle of a café and risk everyone listening in. She also had no idea what she wanted to say to him after his disappearance the morning after the dance.

★   ★   ★

Megan enjoyed her plate of cheese and pork ravioli served with fresh baked bread stuffed with olives. Despite her resolve to be careful with the calories, she could not resist the waiter's insistence that she must try the home-made strudel. It turned out he was correct, and she enjoyed every bite of the warm, sweet pastry accompanied by a creamy latte.

When she left the café the streets were filled with skiers and snowboarders looking for a place to eat and enjoy some après-ski. She decided to head back to the B&B, but not before visiting the bakery and confectioners for emergency supplies of snacks.

Her phone rang as she walked towards her accommodation. It was Giovanni. She had to think quickly — answer now and speak to him in the street, or return to her accommodation and risk losing her signal. She pressed answer.

'Hello, Giovanni.'

'Megan! Thank goodness, are you OK? Have you found accommodation?'

'Yes, I have.' She gave him the name of where she was staying. 'Thank you for your message. I keep losing the phone signal, so it was difficult to call you.'

'No matter just as long as you are safe.'

'I am — in fact I'm just making my way back now for an early night.'

'Good, I'm pleased, sometimes the skiers can become a bit boisterous after a few beers.'

'Yes, I can imagine.'

'Take care, Megan.'

'You too, Giovanni — goodnight.'

'Goodnight, Megan.'

She held the phone to her ear reluctant to end the call, but as she approached the B&B the signal was lost, and the call cut off.

Exhausted after the events of the day and full after her delicious meal, when she reached her room Megan lay on top of the bed, thinking of a dark-haired man with caring brown eyes whispering soft words in her ear.

* * *

A sound from within the house woke her and for a moment Megan lay still trying to get her bearings. The only light in the room came from the streetlights outside the window.

The sound came again, and Megan realised it was the sound of someone laughing in the corridor. She checked the time, shocked to discover it was almost nine o'clock in the evening — she had napped for almost three hours.

She checked her phone; no messages and no signal. She moved towards her bag for a bottle of water, then remembered Clara telling her the bar in the house opened at night for their residents. Dare she go for a drink on her own? she wondered, then answered her own question by remembering the point of her assignment.

Quickly she washed her face, brushed her hair, and put on a smudge of lip gloss. With a final squirt of eau de toilette, she collected her bag and left her room to find the bar.

Clara greeted her like a long-lost friend when she entered the room, which held half a dozen tables, and introduced her to her husband Pieter who appeared to be the barman.

'Ah, welcome,' said Clara. 'Come, take a seat and join in. We were discussing whether Aperol is best served with white wine or prosecco.'

Megan looked around the others, two girls similar to her own age who seemed to be dressed in their pyjamas and slippers with heavy jumpers on top; a middle-aged couple who smiled warmly at her; and a single male with his head in his phone and a heavily bandaged wrist.

'I'm not really sure,' Megan replied. 'I don't think I've ever tasted it.'

'Never? It is the drink of the region! Of course we would have it without anything added,' Clara explained. 'The girls favour prosecco.'

On cue the girls giggled their approval and raised glasses containing a bright orange liquid.

'And we prefer white wine.' The middle-aged gentleman smiled. 'But Eric here, he prefers the traditional way.' He waved in the direction of the younger man, who nodded towards his glass.

Megan realised everyone seemed to be enjoying the same drink.

'Well I suppose I should try one too. Perhaps I'll begin with an original and then decide if it needs adjusting.' Secretly she was afraid of the effect if she added prosecco or wine.

'Brava!' Pieter said, beaming, pouring some orange liquid into a glass.

Megan agreed with Eric, the original tasted enjoyable without any additions. Her fellow guests cheered her opinion and Megan enjoyed a lovely evening in their company.

It wasn't quite the first evening experience with the coach tour she had expected, but Megan wondered if perhaps it had been better.

★ ★ ★

The next two days fell into a routine, whereby Megan, after a full breakfast at the B&B, joined the coach party and followed their itinerary for the day. This included trying some of the nursery slopes for the less able skiers — including Megan — and for others, heading to more advanced runs.

Although not yet skilled enough to move off the baby runs, as she described them in her media posts, Megan felt triumphant at the progress she made, as the cold stung her eyes and took her breath away. Surrounded by brightly clothed fellow skiers, the experience was exhilarating.

Most days she joined the group for a light lunch and discovered that, as she had suspected, although they were lone travellers some of them met up on these tours on a regular basis. She collected their stories and recommendations for use in her articles, wowed her social media accounts with panoramic views, kept them updated on her progress at skiing, and gave feedback on the food and drink.

In the evening though, she was happy to return to the B&B, enjoy her evening meal in the little café she had found on her first evening, and appreciate the company of Clara, Pieter and the other lodgers over a nightcap before bed.

★　★　★

Megan held her breath as Monte Marmolada loomed high above them. They were on the third day of the tour and waiting to travel by cable car to the top of the mountain glacier. As they waited in the queue Megan watched the cable cars ascend and descend and her stomach plummeted. She was really not sure she could do this, and regretted eating Clara's hearty breakfast of pork and apple sausage.

All around her excited tourists eagerly awaited their turn to travel in the car, their cameras snapping incessantly. She really wished Luca was with her today, but he wasn't due to arrive for another two days to complete his part in the assignment.

The cable car arrived and they began to board. She rummaged in her bag for her phone to take some photos when the mechanism of the car caused it to jerk slightly, causing her to lurch forward and then backwards.

'Be careful there,' a voice said as two strong arms caught her.

In alarm she turned around . . . and straight into the arms of Giovanni.

7

'What are you doing here?' Megan asked Giovanni when she caught her breath.

'Well, it's nice to see you too,' Giovanni answered, smiling at her. 'I couldn't settle knowing I was probably responsible for your predicament and so I arranged for cover and headed up here as soon as I could. I checked your itinerary with Luca and knew where you would be this morning. I've been waiting here since the lifts opened to try to catch you, and I did, quite literally in fact.' He smiled.

'I have no need for a babysitter — I'm managing just fine, thank you,' Megan snapped, confused by the situation, She immediately regretted her tone as the words left her mouth.

Giovanni's face fell at the harshness of her words.

'Would you like me to leave?'

But even as he spoke the doors to the car closed and they were enclosed with another twenty or so people in a tin can that was about to ascend hundreds if not thousands of feet.

Megan wobbled slightly and he reached for her elbow to steady her.

'I'm sorry,' she said. 'That was uncalled for. I'm nervous about this cable car. Did you really wait for hours in the cold to catch up with me?'

'Yes, yes, I did. And you are right to be angry with me for many reasons, but this is not the place to talk about such things.' He motioned to the proximity of the others around them, which Megan seemed to have forgotten. 'Let's just enjoy the view for now and we can talk later.'

Megan agreed and turned to the window to watch. They climbed ever higher while Giovanni wrapped his arms around her and held her close, a situation Megan found scary and wonderful in equal measure.

When they reached the top and exited with the others onto the glacier, Megan hesitantly discovered that the spectacular viewing gallery was well worth the journey up in the cable car. Her fellow travellers, reassured that Megan did know the stranger who had joined their group, were happy to leave them and wandered off in their groups to explore.

'How about we grab a coffee in the café? We can look over the whole area from there,' Giovanni suggested.

Megan, pleased to have the chance to sit down after the ride in the cable car, agreed gratefully.

'Yes, please. I didn't anticipate using the cable car would leave me feeling so wobbly or so cold.'

Giovanni offered her his hand to steady her and she happily accepted.

They found a quiet window table where they drank their coffee as they studied the view.

'Thank you.' Megan broke the silence. 'For coming to look for me.'

'I wish I had been able to come earlier. The thought of you trying to find somewhere to stay with night falling terrified me. Thank goodness you were able to sort it all out for yourself, you proved to be more than capable.'

'I'm not —' she began, then softening her voice she continued, 'Well, not really. It's easy to be capable with the back-up of a big company.'

'Yes, a company which let you down,' Giovanni answered as his jaw tightened. 'Due to my relationship with Anna.'

Megan said nothing. Giovanni played with his coffee cup before continuing.

'I feel I owe you an explanation, Megan. It wasn't really a relationship, to be honest. She was one of Laura's friends from school. But that all died out until two years ago when she sent me a message asking me to do her a favour and invite her as my guest to the ball, as she wanted to write a piece for her magazine. I saw no harm and agreed.' He turned back to the window.

Megan reached out to touch his hand.

'You don't have to tell me any of this.'

He turned and she could see pain in his eyes.

'I do, because I don't want you to think of me as someone who plays with

118

other people's emotions, and it explains why I left for home without speaking to you the night after the ball.' He took a deep breath. 'At the ball with Anna as my guest it became clear she wanted more. She acted as though we were an item, and to distract her from that I spent the night telling her the family history and how it was important to me to look after those traditions even though it wasn't my real ambition in life. I just wanted to keep her talking about boring things, especially on the drive home —'

'Stop, Giovanni. I don't need to hear this.' Megan held his hands. 'You don't owe me any explanation.'

'I need to say it.' He tried a weak smile. 'When I stopped the car, she tried to kiss me and I stopped her, I didn't think of her in that way. It all became very unpleasant she threw insults at me and threatened to ruin me and the farm.'

'Which is when the article was published,' Megan said.

'Oh yes, and what an article it was. She wrote that the farm only succeeded because my father married my mother for her family's money. That I was doing a job I hated because I felt responsible for my father's accident and that had led me to become a recluse who hated visitors but that I too needed to wed into money to save the farm. It was quite a headliner in the world of olive farms.'

'How awful. How on earth did she keep her job?'

'Oh, it was disastrous. The negative publicity caused us to lose sales. As you know, mud sticks, and as though that wasn't bad enough it caused a huge fallout within the family. My father threatened to sue the magazine. I have no idea how she held on to her job — for some reason Claudia seems to have a soft spot for her.'

'How very strange. Thankfully your family are close — you've recovered and moved on?'

'Yes, well, that's a matter of opinion. It gave Luca and Laura a get out of jail free card. They were annoyed at being judged for not being involved with the farm and I suppose to make amends and life easy for everyone I tried to play it all down and give the impression I wanted to do it all on my own anyway.'

'And your father's accident?'

'Well yes, I was home from university for the holidays and as usual helping on the farm. My father was working at height on a ladder and I knew he was tired. I should have stayed to steady the ladder, but I wanted to finish a piece of writing, so I delayed going to hold the ladder, and he fell.' Giovanni closed his eyes at the memory, when he started talking again there was a tone of resignation in his voice. 'So, in effect the article achieved the very thing I had been fighting against. Which is why I try not to have long term relationships I just don't have the time to give, and why I panicked after the ball, because I felt there was the potential for something between us and I have nothing to offer.'

'Don't you think I should be allowed a say in that, Giovanni?'

He shrugged. 'I just wanted to nip it

in the bud before things went too far and we lost a friendship.'

Megan sighed. 'Giovanni, I appreciate your honesty. I enjoy being in your company and . . .' She lowered her eyes for a moment before continuing. 'I felt something too, Giovanni.'

Giovanni reached for her hands.

'Where do we go from here, Megan?'

'I don't know. I'll be returning home in a few months. Maybe we just need to learn to value the time we have.'

He lifted her hands and gently kissed them and despite the cold at the top of the mountain, Megan felt heat course through her body.

Before it was time to head back to the cable car, Megan managed to take some photos including one of the pizza menus for her followers, which she posted with the message, *Anyone for high altitude pizza?*

The number of followers, and interaction with messages, impressed Giovanni.

'You really are amazing, Megan,' he remarked.

'Who, me? I'm basically a very junior writer who is in over her head. Watch this space, I'll be down to earth with a bump before long.'

Suddenly realising she was about to step back into a cable car, Megan immediately regretted those words.

Giovanni shepherded her into the car and they were joined by a number of people from the coach party carrying souvenirs and happily chattering about their experience, preventing any further hesitation on Megan's part. Before long the car began its descent downwards.

Giovanni again stood behind her and the strength of him calmed her to the extent she began to enjoy the journey. For some reason it was more pleasurable than the ride upwards. Just before they reached the halfway station the car juddered to a halt, leaving them dangling mid-air. A recorded message advised them this was perfectly normal, and was due to backlog at the station, and they would be moving again soon. Megan's body tensed and a sense of panic rose in her. She felt Giovanni hold her tighter and whisper words in her ear as he turned her towards him to hold her gaze.

As he did so from the corner of her eye, she spotted one of their group, an older woman, grab for the handrail and her face drained of colour as she struggled for breath.

Megan moved quickly; she pushed Giovanni from her and he, thinking she was panicking, tried to hold her until he heard her assertively ask one of their group for the paper bag holding her souvenir. Bending close to the woman who was now crouched on the floor, Megan instructed her to breathe into the bag, hold it over her mouth and keep breathing normally. She spoke gently but with an authoritative air and the woman followed her guidance. Within moments her breathing returned to normal. Megan could hear Giovanni speaking with the attendant in the car and heard him radio to the station at ground level.

As the car started up again, Megan stayed with the woman and kept her calm as she recovered. When they reached the ground station a paramedic team was waiting to attend to the woman, who was well enough to step out of the car, gratefully thanking Megan. The other passengers applauded her enthusiastically for her quick thinking.

Megan smiled in appreciation, but she whispered to Giovanni. 'I think I need a drink.'

Giovanni spoke to the others.

'Thank you, we are just going to get a coffee — she'll catch up with you at the coach.' And the others cheerfully waved them off.

Giovanni put his arm around Megan and led her away from the others, but not to a café, he led her to his car in the car park. Megan fell gratefully into the front passenger seat as Giovanni sat in the driver's seat.

'Would you like me to get you a drink?'

'No —' Megan started to say but her voice trembled. She reached over and he gathered her in his arms and let her give in to the tears.

'I'm so sorry,' she said between sobs.

'Why? Megan, your reactions in that cable car saved that woman from becoming extremely ill and prevented panic. You took control and I was incredibly proud of you.' He smiled. 'Would you like to return with the coach party to the hotel or would you like me to drive you back to the B&B?'

'I couldn't ask you to do that, Giovanni — you have the farm, you're needed at home.' Megan wiped her eyes and gathered herself together.

'Megan, I drive up and down these roads to go mountain biking. I cycle them often. It's no problem for me to drop you off and maybe we could have a meal together and then I can drive home in the evening.'

'It sounds tempting. I'm not sure I can face another journey on the coach at the moment.'

'That settles it. We'll find them and let them know there has been a change of plan.'

It had been an eventful day one

way or another and Megan's body felt exhausted, but there was so much she needed to think over. As they settled into the car and Giovanni started the engine, she closed her eyes for a moment.

'Megan, Megan, is this the correct place?'

Giovanni's voice came from far away. She opened her eyes and blinked at the B&B in front of her.

'Oh Giovanni, have I slept all the way?'

'Yes.' Giovanni chuckled.

'Oh, my.' She held her head in her hands. 'I've not been particularly good company, and you must be exhausted too. If you want to head for home, I don't mind if we don't have dinner.'

Giovanni laughed. 'I actually might stay over with my friends, and travel at first light tomorrow.'

'Can you do that?' Megan was suddenly wide awake.

'Yes, I can, if that is OK with you?'

'Yes! I would feel so much better knowing you weren't driving home in the dark and down those winding roads after a long day.'

'How do you know the roads are winding? You slept through the journey.' Giovanni laughed, then pretended to wince as Megan playfully punched him on the arm.

'Come in with me — you can wait in the lounge while I get changed. I'm sure Clara won't mind.'

Of course, Clara didn't object, especially when Megan told her about the cable car incident.

'And you helped her, oh, Megan wasn't it lucky you were there? Now you take yourself upstairs, and get changed, I'll look after this young man. Sit down, sit down. I'll bring you some coffee.'

She directed her last commands to Giovanni, who sank gratefully into a comfy sofa.

Megan threw herself under the shower, dried herself off and put on fresh jeans and a tunic top, straightened her windswept hair, swiped her eyelashes with mascara and applied some lipstick, which was the sum total of make-up currently in her toilet bag. One last application of perfume and she felt refreshed and ready for eating out with Giovanni.

She made her way downstairs. Clara appeared in the hallway, a finger to her lips. She gently opened the lounge door. Giovanni was sound asleep under a cosy blanket.

Clara indicated for Megan to follow her back into the hall, where she whispered, 'He was asleep before I even brought his coffee. I covered him with the blanket. Why don't we have coffee while you wait for him to wake up?'

Over coffee Megan filled Clara in on their plans for the evening, depending on when Giovanni woke up, and how he hoped to stay at his friend's house before driving home in the morning.

Clara said she had a small room which was unoccupied if his friend wasn't available — or for only the additional cost of breakfast, he could stay in Megan's room. Megan quickly advised her that would not be appropriate on this occasion. Clara chuckled and re-offered the single room if Giovanni changed his plans.

The sound of the phone ringing made them jump. Clara answered as Megan moved back to the lounge to check on Giovanni, to find the noise of the phone had woken him. He sat up sleepily.

'I'm sorry, Megan. I just intended closing my eyes for a minute. I must have dozed off.' He looked at the blanket. 'Thank you.'

'Clara's doing, not mine. Oh, and she says she has a single room free in case your friend can't accommodate you.'

Giovanni took a deep breath. 'I forgot to phone them. I intended to call while you were changing.'

'Look, why don't you go up to my room and freshen up and I'll sort out the room with Clara? I really don't want you driving any more tonight — I feel bad enough to have put you in this situation. Then we can go for a meal and come back for a drink or a coffee in the lounge.'

'I think that would be a good idea, and

then we can both relax.'

Megan smiled as she directed Giovanni to her room, happy to have found a solution and even more pleased at the opportunity to spend some more time with this handsome, complex man.

★ ★ ★

Over risotto and a glass of red wine in the café Megan now thought of as her local, they discussed the events of the day. Megan confessed she was thankful the week was nearly over. Much as she liked the other people on the tour and the experience, she wouldn't miss being on the coach as it negotiated those treacherous roads.

Giovanni laughed.

'You should see it in summer, when the mountain bikers are riding alongside those coaches.'

Megan shuddered at the thought. 'I'm glad I'll be in another part of Italy, well away from them.'

'I'm not.' Giovanni said making a sad

face at her across the table. Then changing the subject, he said, 'You must be tired hearing about me and my family. Tell me about your family, and why you wanted this assignment.'

'Well, I didn't expect it. I thought my boss was joking when it was offered. As it transpired, it turned up at the right time for me, although I still feel like an impostor. My mum and dad are normal parents; my sister is obsessed with sport and winning competitions.' She rolled her eyes.

'My brother — well, funnily enough I think he must be like you, Giovanni. His first love is fashion design and he's incredibly good at it, but my father didn't think it was a suitable career and discouraged him. When he decided to join the police, my parents were delighted. I know he put his dreams on hold to please them, and I'm so pleased he is now pursuing his own ambitions.'

'Then you are like my family, all with different careers and ambitions,' Giovanni said.

'Yes, we are indeed. Although I do think you all have the same creative and artistic ambitions — you just pursue it in different media. I wonder what you could achieve if you could find a mutual project to work on together.'

'I don't ever see that happening. We are moving in different directions. It does make me sad, but the world changes with each generation.'

Megan agreed, then suggested they should think about heading back to the B&B, laughing as she said, 'I have a nightly date with a glass of Aperol since I've been here.'

'Well, that sounds good to me — and who am I to stand in the way of your routine?'

Slowly they walked hand in hand, as though neither wanted the evening to end, stopping to admire far-off lights twinkling further up the mountain. Giovanni turned Megan towards him.

'I'm so glad my brother brought you into our lives, Megan.'

He gently drew his finger across her

cheek and down towards her mouth, tracing the outline of her lips, then tilting her chin slightly he reached down and gently placed a kiss upon her lips. It was so gentle she barely felt the brush of his lips, but the connection was enough to send a delicious shiver through her entire body.

8

'Great work, Megan.' Bob's voice echoed through the apartment from her mobile phone. 'The executive team and our advertisers are delighted. I'm sorry it got off to a rocky start, but you pulled it out of the hat, and that incident with the woman in the cable car — I can't believe you kept it quiet. Lucky for us, your fellow travellers were not quite so reticent. Well done, Megan.'

'Thank you, Bob. I didn't really do anything heroic, it was just something I saw on TV.'

'Now, next up on the agenda.' Bob changed the subject. 'We have the fashion show in Milan. Is there anything you need from us to help you with this next challenge?'

Megan answered hesitantly.

'Well, there is a dress code, Bob, and I'm not sure anything I have with me will do.'

'Say no more. You buy whatever you need, Megan — within reason!' He laughed nervously. 'I'll make sure there's money in the account.'

'Thank you, Bob.'

'No, thank *you*. Now keep up the good work; take care, Megan, and we'll hear from you soon.'

Bob ended the call, leaving Megan relieved he was not a man for making small talk.

She laid her mobile phone down on the kitchen worktop while she finished making coffee. Where on earth would she find a reasonably priced outfit to suit the meticulous requirements laid down by Claudia when she handed her the invitation?

When she answered Claudia's request to speak with her and Anna in the office, following the Dolomite trip, Megan hoped it would resolve any further issues. She squirmed in her seat when Claudia reminded Anna in no uncertain terms to be careful in any further booking as she did not want to be answerable to the UK office again for the incompetence of her staff.

Aware of the tense atmosphere between the two women, Megan tried to distract them by tentatively enquiring what Claudia and Anna would be wearing to the fashion show only to be met by a withering look from Claudia, who was clearly still trying to control her temper.

'Armani, what else?' Anna walked with Megan to the elevator when the meeting ended. 'I'm sorry about the booking, Megan, and the ball. I hope we can start again.' 'Of course. I'm only here to do a job to the best of my ability. Then I'll be gone.' 'Claudia always favours Armani, by the way,'

Anna said. 'Just so you know, blue this year — if you wish to avoid clashing colours.'

'Thanks, Anna — I'll see you both there,' Megan answered, pleased at this apparent truce.

Back at the apartment Megan sat with her coffee on the balcony and wondered where to begin searching for a suitable outfit. Could she chance going back to Claudia's friend Rosario? But she knew her prices were eye-watering, and she couldn't ask for another freebie.

Maybe her brother Ryan could point her in the right direction, of something low cost but passable as a designer piece that would not have Claudia tutting in her direction.

Just for fun she posted on social media a photo of her backpack, with the tagline *Hope I can find an outfit in here for Fashion Week, not holding my breath . . .*

★　★　★

The day Megan dreaded dawned bright and sunny, which seemed in conflict to how she felt. Fashion was most definitely out of her comfort zone. She dressed quickly and hurried downstairs to greet Luca, who was collecting her to drive to Milan. He looked drop-dead gorgeous in his dark suit trousers, open-necked shirt and patterned neckerchief casually draped around his neck.

He whistled when he spotted her, and Megan made an appreciative curtsey in her gold silk trousers topped with a gold organza longer-length jacket with a mandarin collar, under which she wore an ivory-coloured tunic blouse with a ruffled neckline finished off with a gold coloured brooch. Even her straw tote bag had been sprayed gold.

'You look fabulous, Megan. I don't think Claudia could possibly find fault.' He held the car door open for her.

'Thank you, Luca, you look well-groomed and handsome yourself.' She hung her jacket inside the back passenger seat alongside Luca's, not daring to risk crushing it during the trip.

'All Roberto's doing, he has a good eye for pulling an outfit together.'

'Just like my brother. I'm so lucky one of his designer friends, Ami, came up with this.' She reached in her bag. 'I've brought the scarf he designed and made for me. Since he can't go to the show, at least his scarf can.'

'Of course — and I hope you have

contact details for him and Ami as I'm sure you will be asked for their details before the day is done.' Luca smiled as he started the engine and they began their two-hour journey towards Milan.

'Do you really think so, Luca?'

'It's fashion week, who knows what or who will be the talk of the town?' Luca laughed.

'Ryan loves all this stuff. Do you think Giovanni feels obliged to follow your parents' wishes in the same way my brother does?'

'Before I answer your question, perhaps you could answer mine? What exactly is going on with you two?'

Megan shifted uncomfortably in her seat.

'Nothing, we are just friends. Since we were forced into each other's company by your Nonna —' she smiled — 'we have found we have shared interests, and I was grateful to see a friendly face when I was in that cable car.'

'Yes, you told me when I came to take my photos and he stayed over.' Luca raised his eyebrows at her.

'No — well, yes, but no. He stayed in a separate room, you know that.' She pretended to scowl at him. 'As I said, we are just friends.'

'I'm pleased for you, then. My brother is a good man. A serious man, but a good man just the same. The last thing I would want is for you to be disappointed or heartbroken. I don't want to choose between my friend and my brother.'

Megan quickly turned the conversation back to the subject she wanted to know more about.

'You haven't answered my question.'

'No, you're correct — I haven't.' He sighed. 'Giovanni as you know is very passionate about the olive farm. I think, being the eldest, he was around the adults and heard all their stories about the old days and the history of the family, more so than Laura and I who just ran wild amongst the groves. I think it was his dream to chronicle the history and capture it in a collection of books. But then Papa had his accident and without discussion with Laura and me, he gradually took over more of the running of the farm. I think he enjoys being in charge.'

'How do you feel about Giovanni running the farm? Is it something you would have liked to been involved with?'

'I don't really think I'm farmer material.' Luca laughed. 'Oh, don't get me wrong — if needed we help out, and Giovanni has brought the farm into the modern world and made it even more successful. But like everything else it's a cut-throat business these days. I'm not sure he will continue with it after my parents retire completely.' He shrugged. 'Roberto and I also have our future to think about. The cost of living in Verona and hiring studio space is becoming more and more difficult and we would love to adopt a child.'

Megan gasped. 'Oh Luca, that's wonderful.'

He smiled. 'I know, but it's early days. We may need to relocate just to keep work coming in. Oh, and I haven't discussed this with my family so please keep it under wraps.'

'Mum's the word. Or dad's the word — or two dads are the words.' Megan giggled and Luca joined in her laughter.

*   *   *

Megan could not believe how busy Milan was. Luca warned her to keep close to him as the crowd could become frantic at the possibility of glimpsing a celebrity.

They passed security and made their way into the building where they were to meet Claudia and Anna. It was Luca who spotted them first.

'Oh dear,' he said as Megan's eyes followed the direction in which he was looking.

'Indeed,' she hissed back at him as she locked eyes with Claudia who was wearing a gold-coloured trouser suit — albeit with a bright red blouse. Standing beside her was Anna, dressed in a blue dress and jacket.

'I'm sorry, Claudia,' Megan said as she and Luca joined the two women.

'No matter,' answered Claudia. 'These things happen.' But from the look she gave Megan, it clearly did matter.

'I did ask what you were wearing,' Megan said. 'And Anna suggested you were wearing blue.' She looked daggers at Anna, who shrugged.

'You must have misheard. I said I was wearing blue.' She smirked while hiding her face in her programme. 'Perhaps just try not to sit together. Maybe you would be better off sitting with Luca in the photographer's gallery.'

'Good idea.' Megan answered; she already felt like a fish out of water surrounded by all the flamboyance. 'If you could just excuse me for a moment, Luca, while I freshen up?'

She reached the ladies' rest room before the tears that threatened began to fall. She reached for her phone and dialled her brother's number. She didn't expect him to answer, just needed to hear his voicemail message.

To her surprise he answered immediately, and that was enough to set her off sobbing.

'Megan, listen to me; you dry those tears and get back in that room. Do not let her undermine you. Now, do you have the scarf I gave you and someone who can give you a hand to sort this?'

Megan found Luca waiting for her outside. She handed her phone to him and Luca listened as Ryan gave him instructions which he followed meticulously. When he had finished, he sent a photo to Ryan who pinged back his approval.

Together Megan and Luca walked back into the foyer with Megan now wearing Ryan's scarf wrapped around her from shoulder to waist, like a sash, with the gold brooch holding it in place. The abstract pattern of green, yellow, hints of orange and gold in the scarf complemented the colour of the suit while making it stand out as though it had been designed to have just that effect.

'Are you sitting at the back of the room or in your own seat, Megan?' Luca asked as he adjusted his camera to photograph her with the catwalk in the background.

'I am going to sit in my designated seat, Luca, even though my knees are knocking together. I owe it to myself and every lone traveller who will read this article.'

'Good for you.' He gave her a hug.

Megan made her way down the aisle towards the row where her seat was situated, relieved to find the seat next to Claudia still vacant. She made her way along the row and was delighted to see the shock of her appearance in Anna's eyes. As she took her seat, Claudia whispered, 'Well done, Megan. I like what you've done with the outfit — perhaps I should consider you for the fashion department.'

'Thank you. It's my brother's design.'

'Really?' Claudia touched the scarf. 'I love it — perhaps I could order one from him.'

'I'm sure he could accommodate your order.' Megan smiled.

Despite her trepidation, to her surprise Megan enjoyed the show. The sense of drama, theatrics and artistry entertained her. After it came to a tumultuous end, Megan was thrown when Claudia invited her and Luca to stay for after-show drinks.

Megan glanced at Luca, praying he wouldn't accept. To her relief he declined, saying. 'Sorry Claudia — prior family engagement.'

'What a pity, but Megan can still join us. She can travel back with us,' Claudia declared.

'Actually, Megan is invited. My mama would be so disappointed if I turned up without our guest.'

Megan gathered up her things.

'Yes, sorry we need to rush off. It's been an interesting experience. Thank you for inviting me. Enjoy the drinks.'

Megan and Luca waited until they were outside the building before with a sense of relief, they started giggling.

'Oh, my word. That was dreadful, Luca, we shouldn't have done that.' Megan eventually composed herself and reason took over. 'She is paying our salary.'

'No, the company is paying our salary. We have fulfilled our contract. I have photos, you have words, they will get their article, job done.'

Luca guided her through the crowds and promotion stalls. The centre of Milan was a kaleidoscope of colours as they manoeuvred their way through the square.

'I suppose you have a point.' She smiled.

'I do, and furthermore, I didn't lie — we do have a family meeting.'

'We do?'

'Right in front of you, Megan.' Luca indicated one of the stalls.

Megan felt her heart skip as she saw Giovanni, dressed in white shirt, sleeves rolled up showing off his olive-coloured skin, wearing an apron emblazoned with the logo of the farm and talking animatedly to a customer.

'I didn't know he would be here today — he didn't say,' Megan said.

'That's Giovanni, he's a dark horse.' Luca shrugged. 'Come on, let's go watch the master at work, and who knows — maybe I'll give him a run for his money.'

It pleased Megan to see Giovanni's face break into a smile as he spotted them walking towards him. After the events of the day, his stall seemed like an oasis of calm and normality.

'Well, this is a lovely surprise,' Giovanni said, kissing her on the lips.

Megan blushed with pleasure.

'For me too, I didn't know you would be here.'

'Ah, this is what we do when there are events such as this. We are licensed to promote local goods, it gives us some publicity, some sales and the opportunity to add to our mailing list.' He smiled at Luca who had discarded his jacket, rolled up his sleeves, put on an apron and was happily speaking to customers.

Luca saw her watching in surprise. He shouted, 'Megan! Come watch as the Rossi brothers perform their amazing *Olive The Queen Of The Produce* act.'

Megan did as she was told and held her mobile phone to record whatever mischief Luca now had up his sleeve.

The brothers fell into what was obviously a well-rehearsed routine, and before long the two good-looking young men attracted a crowd as they performed the story of *Olive The Queen Of The Produce*. She wondered if this was something they did as children or maybe it was a family tradition; whatever it was Megan saw their joy shining through as they laughed and joked and obviously ad-libbed forgotten bits.

When the story was over, they posed for photos, took orders, and flirted with the appreciative customers as the assistants took payments. Even Megan pitched in to wrap goods and help move things along, much to Giovanni's delight.

As the crowds drifted away and the stalls began to pack up it was time to go home. Giovanni took Megan to one side and kissed her gently.

'I wish I could take you home, but all this . . .' He indicated the stall, and his assistants.

'It's OK, I understand, this is your work. Luca has arranged to drive me home.'

'Can we meet up tomorrow?'

'Of course.'

'I mean like a proper date, for dinner perhaps?'

'I would like that.' Megan smiled up at him.

'Until tomorrow.'

'Tomorrow.' Megan gathered her things and followed Luca back to his car as her heart soared.

9

'You guys were fantastic at the stall, Luca. You just slotted together and worked like a well-oiled team,' Megan said as Luca drove.

'Yeah, we used to have some good times together when we all worked on the farm. Even Laura enjoyed it — she loved bossing us around and organising things the way she wanted them to run.'

'Such a shame we all grow up and lose those feelings,' Megan said. 'We were the same when we helped Mum and Dad in the shop.'

'Ah, but as they say, your siblings know all the buttons to push to wind you up. And sometimes it's OK for a short time, but long term . . .' Luca shrugged. 'And Giovanni doesn't like us to interfere.' He paused. 'But it's a shame your business won't stay within the family. Giovanni would never allow that to happen.'

'Let me get this right, Luca. You want

the olive farm to continue?'

'Of course, it's part of our family history — it just doesn't fit in with my profession. Sometimes I wish it did. But there you are, I need to keep my business going as does Roberto, and Laura enjoys living in Verona pursuing Bruno.'

If the drive to Milan provided Megan with an insight into Giovanni's world, then the drive home left her confused. She reckoned it was best to keep her thoughts to herself. She struggled to balance the joy these two brothers shared with the expectation it was up to Giovanni to keep the farm going for future generations. Then she reasoned the olive farm had been going for generations without her opinion, so she quickly changed the subject.

'Giovanni has asked me out for to dinner tomorrow night,' she blurted out.

'I know.'

'What? How do you know?'

'He asked me if it would make things difficult for me if you two became an item.'

'So, he thinks we might become an

item,' Megan said. 'And would it make things difficult?'

'Don't tell me you are also asking for my permission?' Luca laughed. 'Have I suddenly become a confessor? You are adults with free will, the choice is yours.' Then he added. 'I just wouldn't want either of you to get hurt when this assignment is over. That's all.'

'We both know I'm going home in a few months,' Megan answered him.

'And before that happens you are heading off down south, so you'll be separated for quite a while anyway. Not to mention your stay on a cruise ship.' Luca again lightened the mood.

'Yes, I'm not sure I'm going to enjoy being trapped on a boat on my own at sea.' Megan made a face and they both laughed as Luca drove them towards Verona.

★ ★ ★

'Which one do you think?' Megan asked Laura as she held up two dresses. 'I should have asked where we were going. Maybe a dress is too much. Should I settle for a nice top and jeans? I can't even raid your wardrobe, Laura. It would be too weird to be eating dinner with Giovanni wearing his sister's dress . . .'

'Would you calm down, Megan!' Laura scolded. 'It's only Giovanni, he probably won't even notice. But since you are asking, I like the navy dress with the polka dots. It's classic and will suit any situation.'

Megan held the dress up to study it. 'You see, Laura, you didn't even have to think about it. But you are of course spot on, if you excuse the pun.' She giggled.

'Your brother does not have the same problem when it comes to pulling an outfit together,' Laura observed. 'Luca's photo of you wearing his scarf over your new designer outfit made the fashion news this morning.'

Megan groaned. 'Oh, please don't remind me. I am delighted for Luca and the publicity it brings him, and I'm pleased for Ami the designer and for my brother, but I wish I didn't have to be the model to spark all this interest in their designs.'

'But surely your boss and the company are delighted.'

'They are, and all my media accounts have been going crazy for their details, but it's not what my assignment was about. The sights and places and experiences are supposed to be the story, not me.'

'Well you might not have intended it to happen, but you have become . . . what do they call it? An influencer,' Laura said.

'Don't be ridiculous.' Megan threw a cushion at her and Laura laughed.

'You can deny it all you like but I for one am delighted for you — and Luca too, as he needs this bit of luck to help his profile as a photographer.'

'Yes, I do hope he gets some commissions from the photo, he deserves it. But as for me, some influencer I am, I can't even choose an outfit.' Megan smiled as she returned to her bedroom to change into the dress Laura had chosen for her.

When Giovanni arrived to collect Megan, Laura whistled her approval at her brother who looked very smart in denims, shirt, and dress jacket.

'Where are you two going tonight?' she asked.

'None of your business, little sister.' Giovanni gave a scowl before kissing the top of her head.

'Well I'm not waiting up, so remember to take your keys.' Laura rolled her eyes as she headed to her own bedroom. Then, turning back, with a cheeky grin she added, 'Both of you!'

Megan felt the beginnings of a flush creep up her face. She had never thought about Giovanni driving home after their dinner. Would he be staying overnight in the guestroom?

'I have an early start in the morning, Little Miss Mischief, and I'll be driving home,' Giovanni called after his sister. Megan was unsure if the words were said for Laura's benefit or her own.

Whatever the reason they had the desired effect. Now she knew he wasn't staying over in the apartment, she could relax and enjoy herself without worrying about any awkwardness at the end of the evening.

'You look lovely, Megan.' Giovanni kissed her cheek, a touch so light she wondered if she had imagined it, but the stirring in her heart told her it had been real enough. 'I have booked a table at a restaurant across the river. I hope that is suitable, but if you prefer, I can rearrange.'

'No, you are the expert. I'm happy to fit in with whatever you have planned,' Megan answered. 'I'm a tourist in this city.'

'Indeed, you are.' He smiled and escorted her from the apartment and to his waiting car.

The restaurant was on the bank of the river and their window seat allowed them to watch the huge candles cast shimmering lights across the water.

Megan was surprised at the attention

given to Giovanni by the staff until he explained the farm supplied the restaurant and the relationship went back over many decades.

'Well since you are a regular, I shall be guided by your choice from the menu,' Megan said. 'I am sure it is all delicious.'

'It is, trust me — and I've tried it all.' He patted his stomach, which Megan could see even through his shirt was muscular and without an ounce of excess fat.

Giovanni ordered for them both and Megan joined him in asking for water rather than wine.

'Why don't you just have a glass of wine or an Aperol?' Giovanni suggested.

'Maybe later,' she answered. 'Why do you have an early start tomorrow?'

'Our harvest lasts from September until December. We rest the trees and feed the ground for a few weeks, and then replanting begins. Tomorrow we begin that process.'

'I would like to see how the farm works sometime. In fact, it is one of the items on my itinerary to check out vineyards and olive farms and see what there is to offer the lone tourist.'

'You are welcome to spend a day working with us, but I'm not sure we could offer much interest to a lone tourist. We are mainly a working farm.'

'I would like that.'

'You would? Well I can arrange that for whenever you have some free time in your diary.'

'I'll be leaving to tour down south on Monday and I won't be back for three weeks.' She played with the cutlery as she spoke.

'Oh, I didn't realise you would be away so long.' Giovanni sounded disappointed.

'But that still gives us three days.'

'Yes, it does.' He brightened up. 'Come to stay for the weekend, Mama would be delighted.'

'If you are sure she wouldn't mind, I would love to spend time with you on the farm.'

'If I collect you early on Saturday morning and bring you back on Sunday evening, would that work with your plans?'

'That would be perfect. I can finish off writing up my notes and articles and have my packing done. I'm travelling by train so packing light.'

He reached for her hand, gently brushing her fingers, sending delicious shivers through her. 'I'll look forward to having you close by.'

Megan enjoyed his company as she cleared her plate of seafood pasta,

'I'm so pleased I let you choose, that was delicious,' she said.

'I'm glad it was to your satisfaction. I hope when you return from the south, we can do this again.'

Megan was sorry when the time came for them to leave and head back to the apartment.

'I'll walk you in,' Giovanni suggested when he parked the car.

'Would you like a coffee before you drive home?' Megan asked as she opened the apartment door. 'It does feel strange inviting you in when this is your home.'

'It's your home too,' Giovanni answered. 'But no, thank you, I need to get back.'

'Well — thank you for a lovely evening.' Megan turned to face him.

'The pleasure was mine.' Giovanni took her in his arms. Looking deep into her eyes, he traced the outline of her face with his finger.

Megan could feel her breath quickening and her face tilt towards his. Then his lips were on hers. Gently at first, then searching. Then just as suddenly, he released her.

'I'm sorry, Megan. That wasn't planned.' He stepped back, his head lowered.

'I know.' She moved back into his arms and kissed him gently. 'Goodnight, Giovanni. I'll see you on Saturday.'

He smiled and hugged her. 'Yes, Saturday. Goodnight, Megan.' Then reluctantly removing his arms from her, he turned and left.

Megan fell back against the wall remembering the touch of his lips on hers.

* * *

Following a restless night, Megan rose early. She knew there was a pile of work to complete before she could consider leaving to work on the olive farm, the thought of the latter made her smile. She set to work and the morning flew by in a rush of writing and responding to emails, messages on social media and confirming arrangements for her tour around the south.

Leaving nothing to chance, Megan ensured she either booked the reservations herself or double checked on anything already booked by Anna. In accordance with the plan she would travel by train via Venice, Florence, Rome and Naples and then pick up a hire car to travel around the area. This was going to be a real test for her on her own.

When Megan informed Laura she was going to work on the farm over the weekend, Laura made a face and asked, 'And Giovanni suggested it?'

'Yes. Why are you asking?'

Laura let out a whistle. 'Well, I have never known Giovanni to invite any other girlfriend to watch him work.'

'Maybe no one else has asked,' Megan answered, adding quickly, 'And who says I'm his girlfriend?'

'You just did.' Laura laughed as she poured coffee into two cups. 'Come on, time for a break.'

As they sat on the balcony absorbing the view across the park, Megan asked, 'Do you enjoy your job, Laura?'

'It's OK. I enjoy showing people around the exhibits when it's busy. It can be boring off season, just cleaning and occasional cataloguing. I enjoy seeing Bruno regularly. I hoped I would get to organise more events, but that hasn't really happened. On the plus side, it's handy for the apartment, the pay is OK and in the busy season sometimes I even get tips. Why do you ask?'

'I'm not sure. I guess doing this assignment has made me question my own job, and what exactly I want from my own career. Anyway, what do I need to know about working on the farm?'

'It's long hours and hard work and best avoided if you can,' Laura answered.

'Not something you enjoyed doing, then.'

'I loved the farm, still do — I just didn't feel included in the work that was going on and I didn't want to spend hours helping Mama cook for the workers. When I was young, I used to put on concerts and events for an imaginary audience. Sometimes Anna would come to play too, but that stopped after the accident.'

'After your father's accident?' Megan was trying to work out the timeline in her head.

'No, that was a few years later. No, Anna's mother was killed in a car accident and she never came to play again. It was only when we reconnected later that she returned to the farm.'

'That's tragic, poor girl, I can't imagine how she coped.'

'Yes, and when her father remarried, she didn't like her stepmother. I think that's why Anna makes everyone around her miserable.' Laura shrugged.

'Maybe that's why Claudia is so tolerant of her behaviour — perhaps she feels sorry for her,' Megan suggested.

'I think Claudia knew her mother. I'm sorry I can't remember all the details now,' Laura said. 'So, if you are trying to get me back to work on the farm with you, then no thanks. I would sooner listen to Bruno recite Dante.'

★ ★ ★

When Giovanni called to collect Megan there was an awkwardness between them, which Laura picked up on right away. She sighed, looked at them both and said, 'Just get a room.'

Both shocked, they began to speak at the same time, but Laura held up her hand palm outwards and shook her head. 'Not listening.'

It was enough to break the tension between them and Giovanni picked up Megan's holdall as they shouted their goodbyes to Laura.

'I apologise for my sister,' Giovanni said when they were in the car.

'No need, I love every inch of her as though she were my own sister, so we can apologise to each other.' Megan smiled at him.

Giovanni reached over and kissed her. 'Good morning, Megan. I hope you enjoy the weekend.'

Megan held his gaze. 'Yes, I'm looking forward to it.'

The drive out to the farm was lovely, with cypress trees and patchwork fields of differing shades of greens, browns and yellows.

'Mama and Nonna are looking forward to meeting you again. So, I am just warning you they will be fussing over you, forcing food on you and generally trying to marry us off,' Giovanni said.

'They do know I am only here for a few months, then I need to return to the UK?' Megan answered in the face of Giovanni's honesty.

'They do, but that doesn't stop them.'

He shrugged.

Megan laughed. 'Well, you have to admire their tenacity.' She wondered if this was Giovanni's way of putting a line in the sand on the future of their relationship. She decided to change the subject. 'I've been attempting to read Dante but find myself distracted and impressed by the notes in the margins.'

'Oh, my . . .' Giovanni hit his forehead with the heel of his hand. 'I had forgotten about those. I apologise, yes I did like to note my opinions or thoughts.'

'Well, they are most helpful and very insightful. Do you miss writing, Giovanni?'

'Sometimes. I still enjoy putting thoughts on to paper or on to the computer. I've written a history of the farm just to ensure it's not lost forever, but I would love to have more time to spend writing.'

Megan noticed how his face changed and became more animated as he discussed a subject in which he was so emotionally invested. Then just as quickly the curtain fell back in place.

'If Laura could hear me just now, she would say I sound like Bruno with his obsession.' Giovanni adjusted his sunglasses and indicated the view before them. 'Isn't this beautiful, Megan? Do you have a view such as this when you go to work in your office?'

'No, I don't. This is indeed a very lovely area in which to live and work.'

'And cycle, never forget the cycling.'

'How could I? The image of you in your cycling gear the first time we met is burned in my memory.'

'In a good way I hope,' Giovanni made a face.

'Debatable.' Megan laughed.

When they arrived Megan found herself warmly welcomed by Mama and the dogs and ushered into the kitchen where a breakfast of coffee, bread, cheese and cooked meats was waiting despite her protestations she had already eaten.

'Did Laura make breakfast? That girl cannot cook. Bowls of breakfast cereal, that's all she ever eats.' Mama brushed off her excuses. As she was speaking Nonna was demanding Megan's attention from her seat in the corner.

'She wants to thank you for bringing happiness to her grandson,' Mama said.

'Told you,' Giovanni whispered.

Megan hugged Nonna and explained to her how happy she was to visit her home again, but she would be going home in a few months. Giovanni gave an interpretation to his grandmother and she smiled and nodded and spoke a few words.

Giovanni sighed and kissed Nonna fondly on the head. 'She says time will tell, she's never wrong in such matters.'

Thankfully, Papa entered the kitchen and Megan was pleased the distraction avoided the need for her to respond to Nonna's words.

Papa greeted her warmly. 'Are you ready for a busy day?'

'I hope so,' Megan replied.

★ ★ ★

170

By late afternoon as the sky grew dark and the air cooled, Megan could barely move any muscle in her body without something hurting. She was sure she must have walked every inch of the farm and worked within every building. The farm, she discovered, was huge; it ran to acres and acres of olive trees, kiwi trees, lemon trees, and other varieties of fruit in the orchard and a small vineyard. There were numerous buildings dotted throughout used for the various parts of the production process, or storage. There were also buildings which Giovanni explained were used in the past to house workers or for accommodation during the busy harvest times. She remembered he had explained this to her previously.

'Time to call it a day out here, I think,' Giovanni announced.

Megan sighed with relief. The vision of a long hot bath, pyjamas and a comfy bed floated before her. She piled into the truck with the others and wondered where she would be sleeping, and if it would be rude to go straight to bed after dinner.

They dropped others off in another part of the farm to head to their own cars and homes. Only Megan, Papa and Giovanni remained as the truck pulled into the courtyard.

'Right Papa, we'll leave you to get washed up and let Mama know we'll be in for dinner in, say, another hour,' Giovanni said.

'I thought we were done?' Megan said, and even she could hear the whine in her voice.

'Oh no, we still have all the paperwork to do and the records to update,' Giovanni answered, leading the way to his office.

Giovanni switched on the computers and the coffee pot. Megan lowered herself on to a sofa. The low lights and comfy sofas seemed inviting to her weary body.

★ ★ ★

'Megan, Megan, time for dinner . . .'
Megan could hear the voice, but it

came from far off. Her eyes flickered open to discover Giovanni leaning over her. It took a moment to become aware of her surroundings and then the realisation of where she was made her jump.

'I fell asleep! Oh Giovanni, I'm so sorry. I was meant to be helping you.' She sat up.

Giovanni put on his serious face. 'Sleeping while still on shift, I'm sure that is grounds for dismissal.'

'I totally agree. It must have been all the fresh air and then the sofa was just so comfortable I just closed my eyes for a minute.'

'Forty-five, more like.'

'No! Oh my word, I need to wash and change. But first is there anything I can do to help you with the paperwork? I feel so bad.'

'It's all done. Here, have a coffee.' He handed her a cup, which she gratefully sipped.

'I don't even know where I'm sleeping tonight, I should have checked with Mama.'

'Oh, you're in with Nonna. Didn't she say?'

'Oh, fine. That will be nice,' Megan answered, then spotted Giovanni, trying and failing to hold in his laughter. 'Very funny, Giovanni. I wouldn't mind sharing with Nonna to be fair, she's very interesting and I could discuss your future with her, in one way or another.'

'That could prove dangerous.' He laughed. 'No, Mama has arranged for you to stay in Laura's old room. Although there is always the option of this old sofa.'

'Well wherever it is, I had better get there and get changed for dinner.'

★ ★ ★

Dinner with the family but without Laura, Luca and Roberto was a quieter affair. Mama, Papa and Nonna appreciated her gifts of wine and chocolate. They were interested to hear all her experiences in the few weeks since they last met, and delighted her assignment seemed to be successful.

'Does all this success and attention mean you will be promoted when you return home?' Papa asked.

Megan shook her head. 'I am only a very junior member of staff. I doubt there will be any change to that when I get home.'

'But you've probably already brought a great deal of interest to your magazines, and people will want to read more. I am not very up on social media and the like, but my children tell me you have become extremely popular. It seems to me people like what you have to say and that is a skill. It would be a shame to let that go to waste like so many others do these days.'

He paused, and Megan was unsure if he was still speaking to her or Giovanni.

'I didn't get the opportunity to attend university. I probably wouldn't have liked it anyway.' He laughed. 'My skill was in the land, of reading the soil and the seasons. All my children have these skills if they choose to use them, but they are also blessed with other skills, artistic skills, inherited from their mama. We all find our path in life eventually. Maybe this is your path, Megan?'

Mama interrupted the conversation, declaring it boring. 'Come help me tidy up Papa, and no, Megan, do not offer. You have done enough work for free today. Why don't you two take the dogs for a walk? I'm sure you have lots to discuss about your day, we'll catch up with you before bedtime.'

And with that Mama dismissed Megan and Giovanni and returned to her normal routine.

Giovanni took his mother's hint and calling the dogs, he helped Megan into her warm jacket before exiting back into the night air.

'Do you feel up to a walk, Megan?'

'Honestly?'

'I'll take that as a no, then. We can go back to the office, or we can go to my home. Both have coffee, chocolate and alcohol. The choice is yours, no pressure.'

'Well I am curious to see inside your

place — but that's just me being nosey.'

'It's pretty similar to the office, but with fewer computers. My imagination is a bit limited.'

'Well, let me be the judge of that.' Megan immediately regretted her choice of words.

Giovanni didn't comment but allowed the dogs to lead the way.

Megan was pleasantly surprised. The log fire crackled in the hearth and the lights were low. The house was like the main house, just slightly smaller and cosier. The sofas and throws almost matched those in the office. Bookcases lined one wall with what seemed to be well-loved and read books. The dogs made their way to the kitchen to explore their food bowls and then settled in their beds either side of the fire.

'This is lovely, Giovanni.'

'You sound surprised.'

'I shouldn't really be, but I guess I just didn't really think of this as your home, just somewhere to sleep with the main house still being home.'

'This is my home. I see my family every day, but I don't necessarily eat with them. I like my own space; I have my own friends, and I dare say they enjoy spending time on their own without their adult children causing mess.'

'It sounds an ideal situation,' Megan said. 'And from all I witnessed today, which I know was only a small part of your work here, you are good at what you do, and it runs like clockwork.'

'I have a good team, they work hard. They are well paid in comparison to other farms. I encourage them to complete their examinations and they remain loyal to my family. I can ask for no more. Now what can I get for you to drink?'

'What are you having?'

'Red wine.'

'I'll join you in a glass of red then, thank you.'

He poured them both a glass and sat on the sofa with her opposite the log fire. They sat in companionable silence for a few moments just watching the flames flicker causing shadows to dance across the room.

'I'm sorry if my father seemed to be questioning you back there.' He nodded towards the direction of the main house.

'He's just curious. I must admit it will seem strange going back to my normal day to day job after this, but I have no other option.'

'I'm sorry to hear that.' He looked at her.

'Why?'

'I enjoy your company. You make me see things from a different viewpoint.'

'I do?'

'Yes, you do.'

'In a good way?' Her heart was beating fast as he moved closer.

'In a very good way.' He gently cupped her face and kissed her lips slowly.

She responded by moving her arms around his neck bringing their bodies closer together. And then both dogs began barking loudly at some noise outside. Giovanni tried to quieten them but there was clearly someone outside disturbing them. He groaned.

'I'm sorry something is causing them to be upset. I'll have to check.' He moved towards the front door to let the dogs out.

They ran out barking frantically. Megan heard voices from outside and Giovanni speaking to someone.

When he returned, he apologised. 'I am sorry, it was probably a wild pig. The dogs have got the scent but couldn't find anything. My father heard the noise and came out to investigate too.'

'Maybe I should go,' Megan said. 'Now they know we're not really taking the dogs for a walk and I don't want to keep them up waiting for me.'

'Yes — the dogs kind of ruined the moment. I'm sorry.' He grinned at her.

She began laughing. 'They did kind of, but it doesn't mean I wasn't enjoying the moment.'

'I'm pleased.' He kissed her deeply and passionately before saying. 'I'll walk you back.'

And Megan walked across courtyard, content to feel his arm around her shoulder.

10

Megan could not ignore the butterflies in her stomach. Today was the start of a new assignment. She would be travelling to Naples then picking up a hire car and locating her hotel all on her own.

Luca had driven her to Venice to catch the train which would take her to Florence. If she considered her own family to be concerned about her safety, then Luca's family were ten times worse.

Luca would not be joining her on this part of her trip, although he and Giovanni had given her strict instructions to phone if she needed help, and Giovanni insisted she drive his car around the farm to help her adapt to driving on the opposite side of the road. Megan smiled at the similarity between the brothers, both thoughtful and caring and just as stubborn as each other.

As the train pulled out of the station to begin her journey, for the first time

Megan felt a flicker of fear. What on earth was she thinking, doing this on her own? She wanted to go home, she wanted her own bed in her own flat, and a cup of tea that tasted hot and strong. With a horrible sense of dread, she realised she was feeling homesick — and probably at the worst possible time.

She took out her mobile phone and, in an effort to lift her spirits, she fired off some cheery texts to her brother and sister. Then she uploaded a few photos and some messages to her accounts.

Good morning my Adventurous Single Tourist Friends, are you ready for a taste of pizza from Naples, the actual home of our favourite food? Well I know I am! Join me as we share this gastronomic adventure. More to follow.

She added pizza and grinning face emojis.

Even reading the lovely comments from her ASTF followers and responding to messages didn't give her the same thrill today. It was just that feeling of dread that something was bound to go wrong and she would need to be rescued and her whole trip would have been a failure because she wasn't up to the task the magazines expected of her. Her mind returned to Giovanni's father's words and what he said about using your skills. Did she have skills? Or had luck brought her to this place?

She gave herself a shake. This was going to be an awfully long train journey if she was going to spend it beating herself up.

She reached into her backpack and found Giovanni's book. Perfect! Dante's words would keep her company on her journey.

The day wore on. Colourful fields lay out before her like a patchwork quilt, interspersed with rows of cypress trees and small farms. Occasionally a grand estate would come into view and Megan wondered about the people who lived there and their lives. Nearer to the train stations the landscape became more urban with small towns and villages before rolling back into green countryside again.

Megan eventually changed trains in Rome, the busiest station she experienced on her trip, for the final part on her journey to Naples. It was early afternoon and she was thankful she had time to grab a quick panini and coffee in the station.

The hotel she would be staying in was situated in a winery and she looked forward to spending some time learning about the process of wine making, although she hoped it wouldn't be as strenuous as her day on the olive farm.

She smiled at the memory of working alongside Giovanni, his slow smile when she caught him watching her sending delicious shivers through her body.

The train arriving at Naples station brought her back to earth with a jolt and she gathered her belongings, checked she knew where to pick up the car and with a deep breath set off on the next part of her assignment.

★   ★   ★

Naples was busy, and perhaps not the best place to be thrown in at the deep end, driving a strange car in a strange country. As she pulled away from the hire car forecourt, she felt beads of perspiration run down her back.

Stay calm, keep breathing, she told herself through gritted teeth. Once away from the craziness of the city traffic, relief flooded through her as after an hour of driving, she turned off the narrow main road and after a few more minutes, through the gates of the winery and hotel where she would be staying.

She admired the view as the grand building with its turreted roof appeared before her and as she parked the car, she decided she might enjoy this experience.

Although maybe not as grand internally as the exterior, her room was comfortable, the staff welcomed her warmly and she was grateful to have the option in her ensuite bathroom of a bath and shower. From her window as dusk fell across the valley, she could see row upon row of vines and rich red earth between them.

Her muscles were sore from working with Giovanni and travelling for so many hours, but also from the strain of wondering if all her arrangements would go smoothly. A part of her expected Anna to throw a spanner in the works.

The thought of a long, luxurious bath thrilled her. Firstly, though, she needed to let everyone know she had arrived safely. Somehow her list of people she needed to inform had grown, which made her smile. She sent a group text. *I've arrived, all well.*

No sooner had she pressed send than her phone rang, as she knew it would.

'Hello, Giovanni.'

'Did the journey go well? Is the car safe to drive? Is there a lock on the hotel door?'

'You sound like my father.' Megan laughed.

'I sound like my own.' He laughed back, his husky voice making her feel she would have given anything to have his arms around her.

'Everything went very well. I must admit I felt a bit panicky at first, but here I am. The hotel is comfy, and the staff seem nice.'

'I miss you.'

'I miss you too, but it won't be for long.'

'Too long.'

'It's my job,' she replied softly.

Megan dressed in clean, skinny-fit denims with a white shirt and draped Ryan's scarf around her neck. She slipped on strappy sandals and carried her straw bag to complete the outfit. Pleased with her appearance in the mirror, she laughed, thinking it would most likely be her evening outfit for the duration of her stay.

Just before seven o'clock she made her way downstairs and into the foyer. The same young girl was behind reception and wished her good evening while directing her towards the dining room, where an older man welcomed her and showed her to her table.

Megan was relieved to find the dining

room only held a dozen or so tables, of which around four were occupied. Two with couples, one with a group of four comprising of two men and two women and another with a group of three women. She chose to face the French doors which gave her the candlelit terrace to look upon, although she had trusty Dante in her bag in case she felt awkward.

Her set meal of salad, pasta and fish followed by lemon pie included a half bottle of wine. Megan carried her unfinished glass of wine into the lounge area when her meal was finished. She intended only to sit long enough to empty her glass before heading to bed.

Before long, the three women joined her. They were from the UK and on a short break. Megan learned about the cookery demonstration and wine tasting they had already experienced at the hotel and how they were looking forward to the ceramic painting due to take place the following day, which Megan herself was signed up to join.

When she did eventually head to bed leaving the women to enjoy their next bottle of wine, she congratulated herself on a successful first day and night then quickly touched wood in case she tempted fate. She dialled Giovanni's number and lay in peaceful bliss as she listened to his soft tones when he answered.

★ ★ ★

Thankful her visit to Pompei was on a fairly cool day, Megan imagined this site with no means of shade could be blisteringly hot in the height of summer. She was now into the third week of her trip in the Campania area, and her notebook and camera were bursting with descriptions and photos of the excellent food she sampled. Pizza really did taste amazing in Naples, as she had posted on her social media more than once.

She had toured olive farms, salt farms, vineyards and numerous historical sites, and when she confidently negotiated the country roads and fought her way through the busy city traffic she smiled at her own daring and wished Giovanni could witness her bravado.

Today was a highlight, though, and for a few hours Megan was lost in the evidence of life before Vesuvius erupted, captured forever in the ruins which lay before her.

Lost in the past, it took Megan by surprise to receive a phone call from Claudia.

'Hello Claudia, is everything OK?' she asked cautiously.

'Well it would be if your article which was due first thing this morning was on my desk,' Claudia said shortly.

'My article?' Megan repeated.

'Yes. As agreed. It should have been sent to Anna before cut-off point.'

'I emailed it yesterday afternoon,' Megan explained. 'You should have it by now, or at least Anna should.' She felt a familiar lurching in her stomach.

'She has not received it.'

'Bear with me, Claudia, while I check

my emails on my phone.'

Megan felt her hands shake; she had never missed a deadline. Then she remembered Tracey, concerned about Anna, had set up Megan's emails to include a blind copy to her in the UK office, along with a receipt and read notification. She quickly located the email with the article attachment and re-sent it direct to Claudia.

'You should have it now, Claudia,' she explained. 'As you can see, it was sent to Anna and Tracey yesterday afternoon.'

'Yes, I can see that now. Thank you, Megan. I apologise for doubting your efficiency. I shall speak to Anna regarding this,' Claudia answered before cutting off the call.

Megan breathed a sigh of relief, gathered herself and prepared to head to Amalfi, where the remainder of her week would be spent exploring Capri and Sorrento and possibly sampling the local Limoncello. Although she was looking forward to time on the Amalfi coast following in the footsteps of glamorous movie stars of a bygone time, she was pleased to know she would be on her final part of this trip and was looking forward to getting back to her base in Verona.

Megan found the drive along the clifftop road both exhilarating and terrifying and felt incredibly relieved when the road descended towards the town, where she found her hotel.

She welcomed the cool blast from the air conditioning as she entered the hotel, and found her way to the reception desk, which was quiet, Megan thought longingly of a cool shower after her exciting drive.

The girl checked her in and then to Megan's surprise, indicated there was someone waiting for her in the bar area.

Megan was shocked; who knew she was here? Then a feeling of panic set in. After her conversation with Claudia earlier, had she done something wrong?

Thanking the girl, Megan walked through to the bar, a feeling of dread settling in the pit of her stomach. Her brain struggled to compute the picture before her — Giovanni standing there in a loose white shirt, casual denim shorts and leather sandals. Immediately all fear left her body, and she rushed into his arms.

'Now that is a lovely welcome,' he said when she stopped hugging and kissing him.

'Oh, Giovanni, what a lovely surprise. I've only just arrived. Did you text me? Is everything OK? When did you decide to visit? How long are you staying for?' The questions rolled out of her.

'I didn't text you. Everything is OK. I only decided after our call last night to visit and managed to get someone to cover for me on the farm. I've booked in to this hotel, I hope that's all right?'

'Of course it is. I need to drop off my stuff in my room and freshen up.'

'I'll wait here for you.'

'I'll be as quick as I can.' She planted a brief kiss on his cheek and rushed to find her room.

★　★　★

When Megan returned to the bar wearing a long sundress she had purchased in Naples, Giovanni smiled at the sight of her.

'The sun has kissed your skin,' he said, brushing his fingers along the length of her arm and sending delicious shivers through her.

'And brought out my freckles.' She grimaced.

'Yes, it has, and they are very pretty.' He kissed the tip of her nose to emphasise his words.

'I can't quite believe you're here,' Megan said as they took a table overlooking the Tyrrhenian Sea, where the sun glinted on the boats sailing on the water, like sparkling jewels on a layer of pale blue chiffon.

'Are you pleased?'

'Oh yes, very.'

'Good. I wasn't sure if you would be displeased to have your assignment interrupted.'

'Not when it's such a welcome interruption.'

Megan had in fact pondered that very question when she had gone upstairs to change. This was a solo tour after all, but then she reasoned who was to say that someone travelling on their own would not meet someone or make friends, and enjoy their company while they were on holiday?

She reached over to touch his hand.

'You've arrived at just the right time.' She thought back to her earlier feelings of homesickness and loneliness. 'Thank you.'

After an early dinner in the hotel, as Giovanni had driven down that day, they walked hand in hand in the dusk. The lights of the town twinkled all the way up the cliff top and reflected in the water, giving the whole scene a magical appearance.

'Italy is a beautiful country, Giovanni. Look at all this. It seems wherever I go, there is beauty, lovely people, and good food. Too much good food.' She laughed.

'Well, I am biased. But I must agree. I've travelled to various parts of the world to study new techniques and promote our produce, and I'm always glad to come home.'

'I don't blame you. I miss my home too, and it doesn't compare to this.' She waved her hand to encompass the scene.

'And I miss you, Megan. You've wrapped yourself around my heart, and I know you will be returning home at the end of the assignment, and I can't bear to think of that time.' He pulled her close towards him and held her tight.

And in that magical place with sparkling lights and twinkling stars, and a cool breeze playing on her skin, she reached up towards him and kissed his lips, as all thoughts of home fled her mind. This was now and it was real.

'Let's go back to the hotel,' she whispered.

* * *

For the next few days Megan saw her assignment through different eyes. She visited Sorrento and Capri, ticked off places of interest, kept her readers informed of her progress, enjoyed the sun and fresh food markets, sampled pizza and ice cream. But now her days were merely marking time until evening when she could spend her nights in Giovanni's company. She decided to travel back with him, tenacious in her resolve to wring out every moment of their time together.

Laura raised an eyebrow when they arrived back together, but asked no questions. Megan wondered if Giovanni had told her of his trip.

After a quick coffee Giovanni said he needed to head back to the farm.

'I'll call you tomorrow when you've had a chance to catch up on writing and sending off your reports. Maybe we could meet up?'

'Yes, I could hire a car and drive out to the farm, now I feel more confident behind the wheel.'

'That's something to think about.' Giovanni kissed her and she was reluctant to let him go.

'Speak to you tomorrow, or before.' She smiled knowing she would be thinking of him all night.

'What was that all about?' Laura asked when he was gone. 'Come on. I want all the details.' Remembering she was speaking about her brother, she quickly corrected herself. 'No, just some of the details. Did Giovanni pick you up from the station? And why are you all googly eyed over each other?'

'Don't tell me your brother never told you he decided to visit me in Amalfi?' Megan asked.

'No, he didn't, and this is so out of character. I've never known him to be like this. Megan, I am so happy for you both — my brother deserves some happiness — but it also makes me sad. You will be going home in a few months, weeks even.'

'We can only make the most of the time while I am here, Laura, we both know that.'

'Well he must be prepared to risk that, Megan. I am still in shock at his romantic gesture. It's given me hope, maybe this will inspire Bruno. What do you think, Megan?'

'I think Bruno is perfect, and he adores you.'

'Yes, I think you are right, he does.'

Then they looked at each other and simultaneously said, 'And Dante too, of course.'

11

For the next few days Megan immersed herself in writing. She found working on the balcony incredibly pleasant due to the warmer days and lighter nights.

Bob, her boss in the UK, confirmed the feedback from her trip had been excellent, especially her experiences of the vineyards and olive groves. Again the sales department had been busy with advertisers looking for space in the magazines.

'People really like your opinion, Megan, and the advice you are giving them is just what they are looking for. Now, listen — I know how tiring all this travelling and taking notes of everything, talking to people and all that involves can be, so I want you to take the days before the cruise to yourself. Have some chill time.'

'Thank you, Bob, I'll do that,' she answered.

Giovanni answered on the first ring.

She held her breath after she asked if she could stay at the farm with him for a few days. She wasn't sure if his parents would approve or if Giovanni would think she was too forward. This was totally out of character, but she was content to grab what happiness she could with unpretentious Giovanni.

'I can think of nothing better,' Giovanni answered. 'I know Mama and Papa will be happy to see you again. Have you mentioned me to your family?'

'My sister and brother guessed. Apparently I spoke about you, a lot. I've not told my parents, but I'll phone them before I leave for the farm.'

'Good. I don't want them to think I'm taking advantage of you.'

'I think it looks more like me taking advantage of you, Giovanni.'

'You could never do that, Megan.'

She smiled. 'See you tomorrow.'

'Yes, first thing. Remember we have an early start here on the farm.'

Megan groaned. 'I've just remembered how sore my muscles were after my last visit.'

Giovanni laughed. 'I'll let you off working this time, just you concentrate on your writing.'

* * *

Megan spent the afternoon food shopping. She didn't want to turn up empty-handed; she hoped Giovanni would allow her to cook a meal for his parents to thank them for their hospitality. She decided she would attempt some home baking too to take as a gift just to show her appreciation. She made cheesecake with mascarpone cheese, and custard with a layer of mixed fruit, and an upside-down apple sponge.

'I hope you're not rushing into things, Megan.' Her mother sounded worried as Megan spoke to her while balancing her mobile between shoulder and ear and at the same time packing her overnight bag.

'I'm not, Mum. Giovanni and his family are lovely people, you would like them.'

'But you're coming home in a few weeks, Megan. You have a job to go back to and this Giovanni, I'm sure he has a job too.'

'Yes, on an olive farm.'

'A farm worker? How on earth did you meet him? I just hope you know what you're doing.'

Megan could picture her mother shaking her head and asking her husband where they had gone wrong with their youngest daughter.

* * *

Giovanni's parents and Nonna greeted her warmly. They were delighted at her offer to cook for them and even enjoyed their meal of roast potato skins with mozzarella cheese, and Southern fried chicken, Megan's standard go-to recipes for entertaining friends, and also the home baking she produced. She hoped they wouldn't read too much into her efforts. She certainly wasn't trying to impress future in-laws; only showing gratitude to a family who welcomed her and made her life and work in Italy pleasurable.

During the day she worked in the office with Bobo and Chichi at her feet reminding her of the pleasure of having a pet, and with occasional visits from Giovanni to attend to paperwork.

It felt good to get all her notes and ideas out of her head and spend time really answering some of the questions people had sent to her. It thrilled her to know so many people felt more confident about travelling or taking a holiday on their own thanks to the information and recommendations she made. It also made her laugh out loud at the pizza and gelato comparisons people were posting daily and even how some cafes and restaurants were now advertising their wares, *As Seen On Pizza To Pisa blog*.

The farm surprised her every day as the days grew longer and the sun heated up. The grove increased in size each day, as it blossomed into a rich tapestry of colour.

She enjoyed working in Giovanni's office and her feelings of homesickness had disappeared. When their day's work was done, she made the two of them a simple meal and they settled for a cosy evening with a glass of wine, luxuriating in the opportunity of spending time together.

On her last day at the farm, Megan received a lovely surprise. Her brother Ryan texted to inform her that as a birthday treat for Chloe, they were popping over to Verona for the weekend. They were already booked into a hotel and were looking forward to meeting all of Megan's friends.

Giovanni was delighted for her and looked forward to meeting her family.

'We must arrange a big family meal here at the farm. You know Mama will want to meet them.'

'I can't impose on your family's hospitality again.'

'Well you can explain that to Mama, I wish you good luck with that one.' He laughed as he walked towards the main building.

Of course, Giovanni was right. No sooner had Megan explained her brother and sister were visiting for the weekend than Mama started preparing for a big family lunch on Saturday, which Megan knew would stretch into dinner too.

'Why are they staying in a hotel?' Mama demanded. 'They could share with you in the apartment or here, they could stay here. Tell your mama and papa to come with them. I have room for them here.'

'They can't leave the shop at such short notice,' Megan explained.

'Ah of course, well they can visit another time, you make sure they know.'

'I'll be sure to tell them, thank you.' Megan hugged Mama, thankful that this woman was so generous towards her.

★ ★ ★

Megan picked her brother and sister up from Verona airport on the Thursday afternoon and her siblings were astounded at the change in her.

'You look so healthy!' Chloe hugged her. 'And skinny! How on earth are you so skinny on a diet of pizza and pasta?'

'I never stop working or walking. Today is the exception — today I am driving.' Megan laughed as she led them to her hire car.

'It's so good to see you, Megan.' Ryan hugged her after they had put the luggage in the car. 'This job has done you the world of good, and I don't think you realise how much of an influencer you've become.'

'Oh, don't be silly, Ryan. Me, an influencer? I don't even know how to influence my own thoughts,' Megan answered as she confidently took her seat behind the wheel and drove out of the airport towards their hotel. Despite Mama's kind offer, Megan and her siblings thought it was better they stayed in a hotel which would free them up to enjoy their trip without being dependent on Giovanni's family.

Once they had settled into their hotel,

she drove them to her apartment where Luca and Roberto were waiting to greet them with pizza and wine.

'Luca! It is so good to meet you at last,' Ryan said as he hugged Luca and Roberto. 'Megan has told us so much about you — well, about you both.' He included Roberto in his conversation. 'She says you are both such talented individuals, and I also want to thank you for keeping an eye on my little sister.

'Am I in time for pizza?' Laura walked into the apartment and introduced herself to the visitors.

'I love your apartment,' Ryan said. 'Thank you for making our sister feel so welcome.'

'Oh, she's OK once you get used to her, I suppose,' Laura answered with a wink and a grin.

'Yes, I would second that.' A voice came from the hallway. Giovanni had arrived unnoticed.

Megan kissed him, before, keeping her arm around his waist, she shyly introduced him to her brother and sister.

'I still can't believe you never said just how fit and handsome Giovanni is, and he owns the farm — he's an eligible bachelor, Megan. You've kept that quiet,' Chloe said accusingly to her sister as they ate breakfast in the dining room of the hotel. Luca and Roberto had collected Ryan early and headed to Milan.

'He doesn't own the farm; his family own the farm,' Megan corrected her. Then, smiling, she added. 'But he is fit and handsome.'

'So where do you think this is going, Megan? Don't get me wrong, I'm delighted for you, but is this just a holiday romance? Or do you think you will be able to sustain a long-distance romance when you come home?'

'We haven't thought that far ahead. Except for occasional business trips, Giovanni is needed here so it's not an option for him to move. And my job is in London. This assignment was a fluke,

I'll be back to my normal routine come autumn.'

'Just in time for the cold and rain and long winter nights.'

'Absolutely, so Ryan had better get my room back to normal for me coming home.' Megan tried to be light-hearted, but there was a catch in her voice as she spoke.

'You know, Megan, I'm not sure Ryan will be moving back home. Actually I think he's considering quitting the police force. His business is really taking off and designing makes him happier than I've ever seen him.'

'I wonder what Mum and Dad would say?'

'You always worry what they will think, Megan. At the end of the day his happiness is more important to them.'

'You're right, I'm positive they will support him in his choices.'

'And you too, Megan — they will support you too.' Chloe patted her sister's arm.

'I've missed our chats, Chloe. You

always know exactly the right thing to say.' Megan put her own hand on top of her sister's, then asked, 'Right, are you ready for a quick tour around Verona? I'm quite an expert now, you know.'

The girls shared a lovely afternoon in the city, sight-seeing, eating and shopping. They arrived back at the apartment exhausted and laden with bags. Megan was pleased to see Bruno drinking coffee with Laura and introduced him to Chloe.

'This is such a beautiful city,' Chloe exclaimed. 'I envy you all living here.'

'It gets a bit too hot and too busy in the summer,' Bruno answered honestly, and Laura shook her head at him.

'Bruno is just telling me the arts and culture department are looking at an overhaul of their structure,' Laura said.

'Job cuts,' Bruno clarified.

'Oh, no. I hope you two won't be affected,' Megan answered.

'I think our jobs will be safe but we might become nothing more than tour guides, rather than curators, which is a shame,' Laura answered. 'Bruno is applying for a post at the university as a full-time lecturer.'

'Well, I have faith in you, Bruno,' Megan said.

'Thank you.' He smiled his rather absent-minded smile at her.

'What are your plans for this evening?' Laura asked.

'We're still waiting to hear from Ryan.'

'Oh, I forgot — Luca phoned. They have met up with friends and are eating in Milan tonight. They said they'll meet up back here later this evening.'

'Well they must be having a nice day, that's great to hear.' Megan said.

'And Bruno and I are having dinner with his parents.' Laura made a face.

'So, it's just us for dinner, Chloe. Giovanni is eating at home but might pop in later. Do you want to head back to your hotel and you can drop your parcels and we can have a bite to eat there and come back to meet up with the others later?'

'Sounds like a plan,' Chloe answered. 'Provided we get a taxi there and back.

I'm not drinking on my own.'

'I can drop you off, it's no problem,' Bruno offered.

'That would be fabulous. Thank you, Bruno,' Chloe said and he blushed.

Laura rolled her eyes at Megan and they both suppressed a giggle.

★　★　★

Over dinner Chloe said, 'You know, Megan, you've landed on your feet here. They really are a lovely family and just so helpful.'

'I think it's their upbringing, Chloe. You will find that out for yourself tomorrow when you meet Mama and Papa, not to forget Nonna. You are really in for a treat with Nonna — she'll have you married off before you've left for home.'

'I wish,' Chloe answered.

'No one on the horizon?'

'I've had one or two dates now with someone I quite like.'

'And you had the cheek to call me a dark horse,' Megan said.

'It's early days, Megan, but who knows.'

'Well, I'm very pleased for you.' Megan hugged her sister.

'Every time I see you ladies, you are celebrating without me.'

Megan's heart skipped a beat as she recognised Giovanni's voice.

'I believe you may need a taxi, and I am here to offer my services whenever you are ready to leave. There is no rush, though — I'll wait in the bar until you are ready.' Giovanni bowed politely.

'Aw, thank you Giovanni,' Megan answered. 'That is so kind of you. We're just finishing up, aren't we, Chloe?'

'We are. I couldn't eat another thing, I'm stuffed. So, if you are ready, I am too. I hope the boys are home, I can't wait to hear how Ryan enjoyed his day.'

Chloe didn't have long to wait to find out as when they arrived at the apartment, everyone was there including Laura and Bruno, who had managed to fast-track dinner at his parents.

Megan had never seen Ryan quite so

animated as he was in his descriptions of his day in Milan and also the conversations he had with friends of Luca and Roberto's, who it seemed loved his designs and ideas. Her brother was totally relaxed in a way she couldn't ever remember seeing. She wondered if Chloe was right; perhaps it was time for him to change career.

Giovanni asked Laura if she minded if he stayed in the guest room, to let him enjoy a glass of wine with their guests.

Laura looked her brother in the eyes.

'Of course, this is your home too, but it is not my business if you stay in the guest room all night. And just so you know, Bruno will be staying over too — and that, big brother, is not *your* business.'

Giovanni laughed.

'Where did my little sister go? He's a good man, Bruno — just make sure you treat him well.'

'I know he is, I am very lucky, but don't tell him that.' Laura winked at her brother.

Megan returned from seeing her brother, sister, Luca and Roberto into their taxis to find Giovanni tidying up and no sign of Laura or Bruno.

'Would you like a coffee or a hot chocolate?' he asked. 'The other two have gone to bed.'

Megan raised her eyebrows.

'That's new. I hope my staying here hasn't caused an issue in their relationship, they never said.'

'I'm staying over too, Megan,' Giovanni said. He poured coffee into a cup for himself and then held the pot over the other cup, waiting for the answer to his earlier question.

'I'm pleased, Giovanni, and I really hope you're not staying in the guest suite.' Megan moved towards him and removed the pot from his hands.

'No coffee, or hot chocolate then?' Giovanni asked as he wrapped his arms around her and placed a long, lingering kiss on her lips.

★ ★ ★

216

As anticipated, lunch at the olive farm was warm and welcoming.

Mama and Nonna had produced a huge lunch of prosciutto crudo, caprese salad, spinach con groviera e prosciutto, pepperoni arrosto, sarde al finocchio, olive pate and a selection of meats, cheeses and fresh bread which made an enticing tableau laid out on the big dining table, and the aroma was heavenly.

Papa enjoyed his place at head of the table, praising and nagging his children and their partners in equal measure. Megan felt a sense of belonging when she was included in his praise and criticism. She knew he had all their best interests at heart and she enjoyed this openness while they ate together as a family and how Mama took charge if she felt Papa needed to go easy.

Giovanni took great pride in showing the visitors around the farm, and Megan felt proud to be by his side. She enjoyed seeing her siblings' surprise at how far the farm extended and the number of buildings. When Giovanni showed them his home Chloe whispered 'love nest' In Megan's ear.

As suspected the lunch moved into dinner and another round of eating and chatting at the table, with everyone helping to serve and clear up. Megan and Bruno were the designated drivers. As Megan drove Chloe and Ryan back to their hotel, Chloe posed the question Megan could not bear to ask herself.

'I don't know how you are going to be able to leave all this behind, Megan.' 'I don't know either,' she answered honestly.

12

Megan was sorry to say goodbye to Chloe and Ryan as she dropped them off at Verona airport. Ryan hugged her close and whispered, 'Thank you Megan, this visit has been what I needed in my life.'

'I hope it helps you make whatever decisions you are facing.' Megan held him close. Chloe wrapped her arms around her sister. 'Remember I want to be chief bridesmaid.' 'Oh, you.' Megan laughed. 'I can't wait to get home and be your annoying little sister again.'

As they left her, Megan sighed. Things were changing in a way she had not anticipated when she first arrived at this very airport only a few months previously.

She drove home with a heavy heart but determined to make the most of her time with Giovanni and hoping a resolution would miraculously appear.

★ ★ ★

All too soon it was time to work on the project and liaise with Claudia and Anna again. Megan hoped Anna had tired of trying to cause mischief, especially with this part of the assignment, the cruise.

Despite her trepidation at experiencing her first cruise, Megan hoped it would make for an interesting article and that gave her a feeling of excitement. The only issue for Megan was leaving Giovanni behind for ten days.

She knew this would be different to the other parts of her assignment. There would be no escape route if she felt she couldn't cope, no Luca or Giovanni to ride to the rescue. She didn't think the captain would be very understanding if she decided she needed to get off the ship because she was homesick. But maybe the enforced captivity, as she thought of it, would focus her mind and she would try to put her head and heart on an even keel.

It was a bit of a shock to Megan to find the ship was huge, ridiculously huge, and she suspected she would have more than one occasion of becoming lost while on board.

According to the daily update and leaflets left on her dressing table, there were lots of activities for her to try during the cruise, and she started to relax knowing that at least there would be parts of the day which would give her some content for her articles and blog posts.

There was also a welcome note included in her pack from someone named Pippa, who it seemed was the social convener especially assigned to those travelling on their own and inviting Megan to a welcome meeting in one of the many lounges before dinner.

As the cruise ship did not set sail until the evening, the first trip she was booked on was to explore Venice as part of a group from the ship. She quickly freshened up and after a few false starts found her way to the departure point where she joined a queue of people who were also taking this opportunity to explore the city built on canals.

The excursion covered a great deal in a short time, including a gondola trip, which gave Megan the opportunity to enjoy an experience which she knew she would never have ventured into on her own.

They walked over the Rialto Bridge, with its myriad of shops, visited the Doges' Palace, and wandered around St Mark's Square where the cost of a coffee from the restaurants was an eye-watering price.

Back on board, Megan quickly unpacked before having a quick shower and changing for her meeting before dinner. Nervously she made her way, as invited, to the lounge for the pre-dinner meeting, not quite sure what to expect. Would it be mainly men or women, young guests, or older guests?

It surprised her to find around a dozen guests already there chatting happily to a cruise staff member whom she assumed to be Pippa.

'Hi.' Pippa welcomed Megan as she approached the area where they were seated. Megan felt it was like her first day of school and she was about to be introduced to her new classmates. She took a seat and before too long the group number increased by around another six people.

In total, as it transpired, there were twenty lone travellers who were interested in using the resources arranged by Pippa. Their ages ranged from twenty-something to eighty-plus and the group was roughly two-thirds female. About half a dozen were previous users of the service and half were first time cruisers which Megan reckoned seemed good odds; the service must be good.

It all seemed very well organised and well run to Megan and she happily agreed to join in with the others for their first meal together and to join them on deck later for the celebrations as they set sail into the evening.

From that first evening, Megan loved every minute of her experience on board ship. When they were at sea she spent the daytime on her own unless it was to attend an activity, but in the evenings she joined up with the group to eat and attend the theatre to see a show, or a film, visit the casino or the nightclub.

It seemed like one big party without needing to arrange a lift or taxi home at the end of the evening. Her followers on social media sent a multitude of questions, which she did her best to answer, and her fellow single travellers were happy to assist her with as much information as they thought would be helpful to anyone considering joining a cruise on their own.

'OK,' Pippa said as she gathered her group ready to disembark for the trip to Florence and Pisa. 'Now this will be a long day, so if anyone finds themselves tiring, this —' she handed out the name and address of a café and her mobile number — 'is the place where I'll base myself for the day while the guides show you around. I'm happy if anyone feels they want to join me in the shade.'

Megan discovered why Pippa gave this advice once they set off. She found herself astounded by the amount of sights the organisers managed to fit into the tour. Her camera filled with photos of The Duomo, the Cathedral, The Ponte Vecchio connecting Uffizi to Palazzo Pitti, and Michelangelo's David.

In the afternoon, the group visited Pisa and the famous leaning tower, where they all took the obligatory photo of holding up the tower amidst much giggling. Megan found a stall selling pizza and gelato and with the help of a fellow passenger managed to catch a photograph to post to her ASTF followers, *I've made it! Pizza to Pisa with gelato thrown in for free.*

Megan also visited Rome, Sorrento and Trapani during her ten days on board. She knew she would be returning to Rome later too.

The days flew by and from the moment she woke until she retired exhausted to bed at night-time Megan loved every minute of her experience on board ship and she never felt lonely or pressurised into joining in because she was on her

own, but in quiet moments she longed
to hear Giovanni's voice.

13

Megan expected Giovanni to meet her as arranged, when she disembarked from the ship and was surprised to find Luca waiting for her. Her heart skipped a beat — had there been an accident? Was Giovanni injured and in hospital? She felt her smile of welcome to Luca was pasted on to her face as her brain tumbled through so many other scenarios.

'Hello Luca, it's good to see you.'

'Hi Megan, did everything go OK?'

'Yes, fine, thank you,' she answered. 'Is something wrong, Luca? As pleased as I am to see you, I was expecting Giovanni. I texted him, but he hasn't answered me.'

They had reached Luca's car and he began loading her luggage.

'I'll explain in the car.'

A shiver ran down Megan's spine. Whatever Luca was about to say, it wasn't good news. She manoeuvred herself into the passenger seat and clutched her handbag to her body as though her life depended upon it.

After what seemed a lifetime Luca got into the car beside her. 'Please Luca, is Giovanni OK? What has happened to him?'

'Giovanni is fine,' Luca said in a quiet voice.

Megan sighed with relief.

'You had a visitor call at the apartment yesterday,' Luca continued. 'Giovanni was there — he was filling the place with flowers for your return.' Megan held her breath.

Luca turned to her. 'The visitor was someone named Jordan.'

'Jordan?' Megan exclaimed. 'Why and how did he even know how to find me?'

'He introduced himself to Giovanni as your fiancé.'

'Oh no! He's an old boyfriend.'

'You didn't tell Giovanni about him?'

'Well, no. Why would I? We had three or four dates and then I realised he was not for me, but this was a very long time ago, and he isn't and wasn't my fiancé.'

'Unfortunately, Giovanni believed him and now he feels a bit foolish. He thinks you are using him while you are here and are just waiting to return home to pick up your life with your boyfriend.'

'But that's not true, Luca. We only went out for a few dates, nothing serious.'

'I believe that, but my stubborn brother doesn't. He's hurting and doesn't want to see you.'

Megan felt as though she had been punched in the stomach.

'Really? He doesn't even want to hear my explanation?'

'Nope.'

'And what about the rest of the family, Luca?' She could feel hot tears prick her eyes as she feared these lovely people who had welcomed her into their family would now think badly of her.

'Megan.' Luca turned to take her in his arms. 'I know the truth, and in time the others will know it too. It's just a bit of a shock with this man turning up.' He let her cry for a bit. 'He's booked into a hotel and wants to meet up with you. That was the message he gave Giovanni.'

Megan groaned. No wonder Giovanni was upset.

'But how did he find me? None of my family would have told him where I was, and why after all this time, does he even think I want to see him?' Megan dabbed at her eyes with a tissue.

'I believe he called in at Piccolo Mondo's office to surprise you —' Luca started to say.

'And Anna gave him my address,' Megan finished for him.

'Well, someone did.'

Megan found a text on her phone from Tracey saying *Phone me when you get this message*. Megan couldn't face speaking to her, it would have to wait. They drove back to the apartment in silence, Megan lost in her thoughts and Luca giving her time and space to process all that had occurred.

Laura was home from work, having lunch when they arrived, and Megan wondered if that was more by arrangement than coincidence. Whatever the reason, Laura took Megan in her arms when she entered the apartment and Megan felt a weight lift from her shoulders.

'Oh, Megan, I am so sorry my idiot brother is behaving like a baby.' Laura exclaimed. 'Thank you, Laura. I'm sure it's just a misunderstanding.'

Laura gave one of her eye rolls. 'Stupid man,' she continued. 'The other one, the overconfident one, left his phone number. He said he's been leaving you messages, but you've not got back to him. He goes home tomorrow.'

'I blocked his number when I finished with him. I don't want to meet up with him. Do you think he's become some sort of a stalker?'

'Maybe you should meet, just to make it clear. Perhaps your success on social media has prompted this visit,' Luca suggested.

'Do you think it has? Why?' Megan asked.

'If he's a social climber, maybe he

thinks you can be useful to him.' Luca shrugged.

'I've not changed. Why would he think that?' Megan asked, bewildered.

'Oh, Megan, you really have no idea how popular your articles have become.' Luca laughed. 'And that's why we love you, you are so unpretentious.' He hugged her.

'Arrange to meet him here. Luca and I can be on hand to support you,' Laura suggested.

'That's a good idea. You are in control of the meeting then, and he already knows you live here so you're not giving him any information he doesn't already have,' Luca agreed.

'You are both right and the sooner I get this sorted the sooner Giovanni will understand it's all been a mix-up. I'll send him a text, I'm not risking speaking to him on the phone,' Megan said.

'Use mine.' Luca handed her his phone and at that moment, Megan rejoiced in her good fortune to have found such a good friend.

* * *

Megan sat nervously awaiting Jordan's visit. Luca and Laura were in the kitchen chattering about their displeasure with their brother. Giovanni had still not answered her calls or texts and she desperately wanted to see him to give him an explanation. She was so lost in thought that she jumped when the doorbell rang, and Luca rushed past her to answer. Laura joined her in the lounge and indicated for Megan to stay seated.

They could hear words coming from the hallway and then Luca ushered Jordan into the lounge.

Megan made to stand up, but Laura placed a gentle hand on her arm, and she stayed seated.

'Megan, you look fabulous. I thought we could have a chat, you know. I've missed you. Can we go somewhere private? Maybe drink or dinner back at my hotel.'

He moved towards her, then stopped

233

as he realised she wasn't rising to greet him.

'I don't know why you're here.'

'I've just said, Megan. I hoped we could get back together again.'

'Why?'

'Because I've missed you.'

Megan sighed. 'I have no intention of having a drink or dinner with you. I told you we were finished and I blocked your number. Are you really so stupid that you can't get that message?'

A sound at the door stopped Megan from speaking further as she looked up expecting to see Giovanni, only to be disappointed as Roberto and Bruno entered the room.

'Everything OK here?' Roberto asked.

'Yes, thank you,' Megan answered. 'I believe Jordan is just leaving.'

'Let me escort him out of the building, then.' Roberto offered.

Megan watched as big, gentle Roberto made it clear there was no further room for discussion as Luca and Bruno moved to follow them.

When the apartment door closed Megan turned to Laura and buried her head in her shoulder and cried, tears of relief and heartbreak. She had been so happy and now Giovanni was lost to her.

★   ★   ★

The following day Megan marched into the offices of Piccolo Mondo. She was in the mood to have it out with Claudia about Anna and her mischief-making. Without preamble she headed straight for Claudia's office.

Claudia looked up from her desk slightly surprised at Megan's unannounced entrance, but her face remained unmoved.

'I'm sorry to barge in unannounced,' Megan said, even though her body language indicated otherwise.

'It's OK, I needed to speak with you, and this is better face to face.' Claudia moved her hand towards the nearby chair for Megan to take a seat.

'What did you want to speak to me

about?' Megan asked.

'To apologise.'

'About Anna, I take it? That's why I'm here. This is the last straw, Claudia. Do you know she gave my address to a stranger?'

'She didn't.'

'She did.'

'No, you misunderstand, Megan. I know she didn't because it was me who gave the address, and I am so very sorry.'

Megan sat open-mouthed.

'Let me explain, Megan,' Claudia continued. 'The man came into the office explaining he had arrived for a short break and wanted to surprise you, but he had mislaid your address. Anna came to ask my advice because she did not want to disclose where you were staying to a stranger, even though he insisted he was your fiancé.' Claudia paused. 'I phoned Bob to ask who this person was and did you know him. Bob said he was indeed your boyfriend.'

Megan let out a sigh remembering Jordan had once accompanied her to a work event. He was in her life for so short a time, it never occurred to her to inform Bob she had ditched him shortly after the event.

'After he had left Bob phoned back. He was in a panic; apparently he'd spoken with someone in the office. Tracey, I think.'

Megan nodded, remembering the missed call from Tracey and imagining the scene in the office as Bob realised his mistake.

Claudia continued. 'And after that conversation he realised the dreadful mistake he'd made. I phoned Luca to explain as I didn't want a stranger turning up at his sister's apartment. I really can't tell you how sorry I am, and I fully understand if you want to make a formal complaint.'

Megan didn't know how to answer except to say, 'You have no idea of the harm this has caused, Claudia.'

'I am so very sorry and I fully understand if you want to end the contract you have with us and return home.'

'No.' Megan answered more loudly than she intended. 'It's a mess but I'll try to sort it out, but I definitely don't want to leave the job undone.'

'Think it over, Megan, the option is there. One other thing if you do wish to complete the contract — I would like you to take Anna with you to Rome.' Megan groaned. Could this day get any worse? 'Why, Claudia? You know we rub each other up the wrong way.'

'I want her to learn from you.' Claudia rearranged the papers on her desk before continuing. 'I was a friend to her mother and I know Anna has lost her way a little and it shows in her behaviour some-times, but I have a gut feeling she has so much more to offer. I can't get through to her but, I think you could, and maybe encourage her. Just remember she didn't give out your address, which she could easily have done and then denied it. I think you've already had an influence on her in a good way.'

'Can you give me a day to think about it?'

'Of course,' Claudia agreed. 'One more thing, and you might like this, Eduardo would like to speak to you about some other writing work.' She lifted the phone receiver and asked Eduardo to come to her office.

From the conversation that followed it appeared a publishing contact of Eduardo had become interested in Megan's work. He liked the style and her attention to detail and how it connected with the reader. He wanted to offer her the opportunity to work on a bigger piece of work, possibly a series of books.

Megan thanked Eduardo for the offer and said she would give it careful consideration. When he had left the room, she turned to Claudia.

'I think he must have mixed me up with someone else.'

'Don't underestimate yourself, Megan,' Claudia answered.

Megan walked back to the apartment with a heavy heart. Not even the gladiators cavorting outside L'Arena could bring a smile to her face.

Within the next few weeks, she had a trip to Rome with Anna to look forward to, and she really didn't see how they could survive together for more than a few hours. But first she would have to phone Chloe and Ryan to explain to them that it turned out her romance with Giovanni was nothing more than a holiday fling.

As she walked, she felt hot tears fill her eyes as she realised she probably would not even see Giovanni again — it was over.

She heard someone shout out before she felt pain and then darkness overcame her.

* * *

'Megan, can you hear me?'

Megan could hear a voice, but she just wanted to retreat back into the darkness again.

'Megan, please wake up.' The voice was pleading and determined not to give her peace.

'Megan, please.' Someone was holding

her hand so tightly it hurt.

With an effort she opened her eyes a tiny crack, just to see who wouldn't let her sleep.

'Nurse, nurse! She's coming round.'

'Is she going to be OK?'

She knew that voice and her eyes filled with tears.

'Giovanni?'

'Yes, my sweetheart, I'm here.' He came to her side immediately.

'I'm sorry, Giovanni, I'm sorry.' She sobbed.

'No, my darling, it's I who am sorry. This is my fault. Can you forgive me?' He held her hand to his lips and placed a gentle kiss on it.

Her eyes grew heavy again and she heard a female voice say, 'Let her sleep now. She's out of danger, she just needs to rest.'

★　★　★

Megan woke again a few hours later with a blinding headache and an awareness

241

she was in a hospital bed.

'Megan! How are you feeling?'

She turned towards the voice, delighted to find Laura at her bedside.

'I'm not sure, really. What happened to me?'

'You were knocked over by an out-of-control scooter. Not your fault. You banged your head when you fell and lost consciousness,' Laura explained.

'I had been at the office.'

'Yes! Well done, that's great you remember.'

'I was upset and angry.'

'Claudia did mention that. I think she feels responsible.'

'I probably wasn't concentrating as I should have been. Thank you for sitting with me.'

'Oh, I've just arrived. There's someone else who's been sitting with you — he's just popped out to get me a coffee.'

And right on cue just as Megan was about to ask who her other visitor was, not daring to believe, Giovanni appeared in the doorway. His face was taut with concern, but his eyes lit up when he saw she was awake.

'Megan, oh Megan, I'm so sorry.'

He rushed towards her as Laura quietly slipped out of the room.

★ ★ ★

'I'm absolutely fine, there is no need for fuss,' Megan protested from the comfort of the sofa in Giovanni's lounge.

'You have to rest, that's what they said at the hospital. You were lucky to escape with just some cuts and bruises and not broken bones — but you did sustain a head injury and that needs rest.'

Giovanni kissed her forehead.

'Yes, to take things easy — not to be totally wrapped in cotton wool,' Megan protested. 'It's bad enough that all my work has been put back two weeks. And that my mother and father are currently living in your parents' house while they make sure I'm OK.'

'And enjoying every moment of it, I might add.' Giovanni laughed. 'They were so worried when they arrived at the hospital, Megan,' he added soberly, remembering Mr and Mrs Hopkins' strained faces as they were ushered in to see their daughter.

'It was a bump on the head, the tests were fine, and I'm fit to return to work. The doctors told me so. I'm so embarrassed by all the fuss.'

'Let people fuss, Megan, it shows they care and that they love you. That I love you, Megan.' He bent down and kissed her softly. 'I love you so very much and I'm sorry I hurt you.'

Megan quickly placed her finger on his lips, thrilled to hear Giovanni speak those words.

'We were both a bit foolish but that's behind us.' She kissed him.

14

Despite her misgivings about working with Anna, Megan found herself relieved to be preparing to head to Rome. Just to be back working was a relief after her enforced recuperation period, and the fuss from her parents and just about everyone else.

She still felt confused as to Claudia's motives behind the suggestion . . . well, not so much a suggestion as an order.

When she asked Luca his opinion on the decision, he shrugged and said he had heard on the grapevine that Anna was on her last warning with Claudia. Megan knew that a dissatisfied, sullen and resentful Anna would not make the ideal travelling companion and decided to be prepared to be on the lookout for trouble.

She felt relieved to know that Luca would be coming with them and the plan was for them to meet up with a group of tourists who were spending the week in Rome. Her short tour of Rome during her cruise, when the ship docked in Civitavecchia, had given her a tantalising taste and she was eager to find out more about this city. They would be based in a central hotel and taking in many of the sights the city had to offer, which were numerous and varied, according to the blurb sent to her by the company who organised the trip.

Megan and Luca travelled together by car. Anna declined a lift, preferring to travel by train and meet up with them at the hotel. Megan didn't encourage her to change her mind, which was out of character for her, but she anticipated that the week would be tricky enough without enduring a long car journey with an unpredictable Anna in the back seat.

'This is your last assignment, Megan. How does that make you feel?' Luca asked her as they headed out of Verona.

'Incredibly confused to be honest.'

'How so?'

'I'm almost pleased it's over, because

then I know I've completed what I set out to do. When I agreed to the project, I didn't know if I could actually do the job. You saw me that day we met in Bob's office — I didn't have a clue what the project entailed, not really.'

'I disagree. I saw a woman who had been badly treated, but who could see a future for herself, who was willing to take the risk even if she failed, who took in the news that another magazine would be involved and adapted her plans. And most importantly, I saw a woman who not only embraced the project but enhanced it and made it her own.'

Megan turned towards him, her eyes open in amazement.

'You saw all that? I can assure you I didn't feel any of it. My knees were shaking I wanted to run out of the office. I felt Bob was making me become a grown-up before I was ready, and I was convinced my colleagues would resent me for landing a free Italian holiday —' She stopped for breath and continued as she remembered. 'Oh — and added to that, the handsome Italian man standing in front of me was going to be my escort.'

Luca roared with laughter. 'Sorry to disappoint you on that score.'

'Just as well you had a handsome brother at home,' Megan answered joining in his laughter

'And that brings me back to my original question and your answer. You said you were confused.'

'Yes, well I think you know the answer to that question, Luca. I love your brother. How can I go home and continue with my life while he's here in Italy? I know people talk about long distance romances, but I am sure they at least intend being in the same place at some point in their lives. How would that work for us — a weekend here and there?'

'I get where you are coming from. Giovanni can't exactly move the farm to the UK, and that's where your career is based. It's a problem for you as a couple.'

'It certainly is.' Megan slumped into her seat, then to steer the conversation away from her and Giovanni she asked, 'How are things with you and Roberto?'

'As a couple we are doing great. For Roberto as an artist, it's a tough world out there.'

'I'm sorry to hear that Luca.'

'Yes, he just needs somewhere to showcase his work but it's an expensive business.'

'I can imagine.' Megan nodded. 'And Laura has work issues too, and Giovanni works night and day to keep the farm going. It seems we are all stuck on the hamster wheel of working to just survive. If only every job could be as pleasurable as this one.'

'Yes, it's been fun. I've enjoyed us working together,' Luca answered. 'I wish we could have worked on some more projects.'

Megan suddenly sat up in the car remembering the conversation she'd had with Eduardo and repeated it to Luca.

'I had forgotten about it until just this moment! It was the afternoon I met with Claudia and just before I ended up in hospital. It must have slipped my memory.'

'Wow! It sounds interesting,' Luca replied. 'Are you going to take it on?'

'I don't think I could do it justice, but I did suggest you as the photographer, if I were to take it on. I hope that's OK.'

'Of course — thanks for thinking of me.'

'Gosh, I had totally forgotten about it. I said I would get back to him when I had given it some consideration. He'll think I'm so rude.'

'Eduardo knows you were in hospital. I'm sure he'll make his friend aware you might take longer in getting back to him.'

Arriving at their hotel, they found Anna sitting in the lounge.

'Well, you two took your time getting here,' she greeted them sullenly.

'Have you found our tour group?' Megan asked, aware that Anna was being watched by a younger man lounging beside a pile of luggage and leaning against a pillar.

Anna huffed. 'That's our group over

there.' She pointed in the direction of a group of UK tourists who were huddled around reception.

Megan noted the group were of mixed ages, from children to seniors and every age in between.

'Have you checked in yet?' Megan asked.

'No, they wouldn't let me without the rest of the group.'

'Well, maybe we should join the group,' Megan suggested as she and Luca made to move towards the reception desk.

What happened next took place so quickly, Megan struggled to get the words out of her mouth. 'Look out!' she shouted at Anna who was checking her mobile phone.

It was too late. The bag snatcher, the man casually standing at the pillar, moved with lightning speed and grabbed Anna's handbag which she had left sitting on her suitcase. He ran outside before he could be stopped.

Luca set off to chase after him but it was too late, the thief had disappeared into the crowded streets.

Megan tried to comfort Anna, who had gone completely quiet. While the hotel receptionist phoned the Polizia, she could feel the eyes of the tour guide burning into her, clearly angry to have his group of tourists exposed to a crime taking place before their eyes on the first day of their holiday.

The members of the group for their part did express concern for Anna and muttered amongst themselves, 'What a pity for the young girl to have been robbed, and right under their noses. The poor soul looks to be in shock, maybe a brandy would help?'

Megan reassured them. 'It's been quite a shock, but we'll take care of our colleague, thank you, I do hope this incident doesn't spoil your enjoyment of your holiday.'

'Oh, you're British,' one lady observed. 'Well, don't you go worrying about us, just look after that young lady.' She patted Megan on the arm.

'Thank you.' Megan smiled gratefully

at her.

Turning to Anna and Luca she said, 'I think our rooms are ready now. Let's get upstairs and sort out whatever we need to do next.'

★ ★ ★

The remainder of Megan, Anna and Luca's afternoon involved giving details of the incident to the police, cancelling Anna's bank and credit cards, reporting her passport stolen and dealing with an angry Claudia. Megan felt thankful that she had prepared herself for just such a situation, and knew exactly what needed to be done.

Megan and Anna were sharing a room, a detail Megan had been unaware of until they booked in. However she reasoned that, given the circumstances, it was probably for the best. Luca's room was situated directly across the hallway.

'Anna, how are you feeling?' Megan asked. She didn't recognise this subdued girl who sat before her. 'Do you need me to call a doctor? Or would you like to go home? You've had a nasty shock.'

'No!' Anna almost shouted. Then in a quieter voice, 'No, thank you.'

'Well, what about family? Is there someone you would like me to contact?'

'No one that would care.'

'I don't believe that, Anna. There must be someone.'

'Only Claudia, and now even she's fed up with me. The people in the office, they hate me, and my work isn't as good because I never have anyone to teach me, I spend all day processing invoices and admin tasks. And now I can't even accompany you without there being a drama.' Anna flapped her hands in frustration.

'Why do you stay in this job if you're not happy, Anna? I don't understand.'

'Because I want to be a writer,' Anna sobbed. 'It's the only thing I have left to me. You wouldn't understand, you've got your family, and now you have Giovanni's family too. But me, I'm alone. My father isn't interested in me now he has a new family. Claudia tries to help, but I'll never be good enough. I do not try to be unpleasant, I just get so angry and envious because life works out for everyone else except me. I even get mugged in full view of everyone.'

Megan held her close and let her cry, sensing the shock of the robbery seemed to have unlocked something inside the girl.

'Oh my gosh Anna, how long have you been coping with all that hurt? You are correct, I have absolutely no idea what you've been through in life, and maybe you weren't offered the support or help you should have been. But it's not too late. If I were you, I would ask Claudia whether the company could offer you access to support to process your trauma.'

'I don't need that kind of help,' Anna answered defensively.

'I disagree, Anna. I think you need support. It's not your fault you lost your mother, or that your father remarried, but it seems to me you want to hit out and punish the world.' Megan held Anna at arms' length and looked straight into her face. 'But by doing so, the only person getting more and more hurt is you.'

'I know, Megan. But I don't know how to stop. I don't even like myself, how could anyone else?' Anna dabbed at her face with a tissue.

'You put a stop to it by being kind to you. By recognising your own worth, and not allowing people to treat you any less. Trust me, I know what I'm talking about in that respect.'

'The visitor who came looking for you?'

'Exactly, he didn't respect me. I don't think I ever thanked you for not giving him my address.'

Anna shrugged. 'I didn't like him.'

Megan laughed. If only you were my friend before I got engaged to him, you would have saved me a lot of heartache.'

'Friend?' Anna asked.

'Well it occurs to me that if you want to have friends then you need to be a friend, and I would like to be your friend if you let me.'

Through tears, Anna nodded.

'Yes, I would like that very much.'

'Just answer me one thing, Anna. What happened between you and Giovanni?'

Anna wiped tears from her face.

'Nothing happened. I guess I thought if I threw myself at him, I could make him fall for me, and when that didn't work, mainly because Giovanni is a gentleman, I stupidly took my revenge on him and the whole family. Then I got into more trouble and blamed him even more. He didn't deserve my behaviour towards him, I think in some way I wanted him to pull me into line.'

'Like a big brother?' Megan offered.

'Exactly.'

'So, tell me, where do you see yourself and your writing career this time next year?'

'I want a project like yours,' Anna replied.

'Sounds good, but do you think the publishers will repeat this project so soon? I got lucky, Anna. I was working the copy desk and doing occasional features. This came out of the blue for me.'

'I don't even get occasional features to practise on. When you go back to the UK, is that what you are going back to doing?'

'Yes, I dare say. I don't really know.' Megan shrugged. 'But I've had a thought — why don't we write up this project together? Show Claudia what you can really do.'

'Really? Do you mean it?'

'I do, Anna. Someone told me recently that I underestimated what I could achieve, and now I'm saying the same to you. I think this could be a new beginning for you.'

'Do you think I could really make a fresh start?' Anna asked.

'I do. Everyone has that choice. Why don't you freshen up and come downstairs for something to eat?'

However Anna declined, choosing to stay in her room for the remainder of the evening.

'I'm tired, Megan. It's been quite a

day. You and Luca go have something to eat, I'll be fine in the morning,' she insisted.

Megan herself felt exhausted by the events of the day and would happily have crawled into her own bed. She reasoned however that Anna maybe needed some time alone to allow her to process all that had happened.

★ ★ ★

Megan joined Luca at their table.

'How is Anna?' he asked.

'Exhausted — but in a strange way I think this could be a turning point in her life.'

'I hope so, Megan.'

'How is the young girl?' Some members of their tour group interrupted them, anxious to be reassured about Anna's welfare.

Megan smiled gratefully at them.

'Thank you all so much for your concern. She's still a bit shaken and so she has decided to have an early night.'

'Do her the power of good. Hopefully she'll be right as rain tomorrow.'

Megan and Luca ordered their meal, Luca convinced Megan to try Suppli al telefono, which to Megan's surprise were rice rissoles, in a meat sauce, with chunks of mozzarella dipped in bread-crumbs and fried in olive oil. They were exactly what she needed.

Luca laughed as she cleared her plate using the last of the bread from the bread basket.

'Did you enjoy that?'

'It was delicious, but I couldn't eat them every day. My waistline couldn't handle it.'

'Do you think Anna will be OK for the remainder of the trip?' Luca asked.

'I think so. We've had a good talk, and agreed she will have a more active role in doing the writing.'

'Wow.'

'Yes, wow. I think she is capable of so much more, and I would like her to have this chance.'

'Do you trust her?'

'I have to; we're sharing a room. Right now, she could be pouring my toiletries down the sink or tossing my clothes out the window.' She laughed nervously. 'I think she has been through an awful lot in her life, mainly unsupported. She expects people to hurt her and so she hits out first. Maybe she just needs to learn to trust again.'

'I didn't realise psychology was another of your skills, but I think you've hit the nail on the head.'

'Not psychology, just common sense. And while I'm on the theme of common sense —' She hesitated and moved her glass around the table.

'Go on,' Luca said. 'I have a feeling I'm not going to like what you're about to say.'

'It's just a thought I've had mulling around in my head and I've not discussed it with Giovanni just in case you think I've been discussing your business with him.' She leaned forward towards Luca, seeking to catch his eye, determined that he should believe her.

'OK, I believe you, go on.'

'Well, you've told me Roberto needs room to display his work, and while I've been visiting vineyards, and olive groves and all sorts of rural attractions around the country, it struck me there is a great deal of business to be made from the additional experiences some of them offer. Such as activities, painting, ceramics, musical entertainment, bed, and breakfast. There's a whole range . . .'

Luca interrupted her.

'Giovanni would never agree.'

'I'm only an observer but I think you could be wrong there,' Megan answered. 'Anyway, that wasn't my complete suggestion.'

'Go on.' Luca stirred his espresso. 'Am I going to need a few more of these or something stronger?'

'You guys are struggling to find premises and you have the ideal location and property right under your noses. Why don't you consider renovating one of the barns or buildings? Roberto could have his gallery, you could have your studio and you could have a home to raise your family. Don't tell me the farm isn't an ideal place to raise a child — and a further bonus for you would be on-site babysitting.'

'I don't see Giovanni agreeing to all that disruption.'

'The way I see it, the farm belongs to all of you, and if you want it to continue, maybe you need to diversify. I get that you and Laura don't want to be involved in the day-to-day farming, but with the size of the farm and the need for people to be offered entertainment or an experience these days, this is where you could be involved. To me it's a win-win solution.'

She drew a breath and leaned back in her seat.

'You have been doing a lot of thinking.' Luca let out a sigh.

'I have a lot of time on my own. And I have another idea.'

'I don't think I can handle any more.' He laughed, holding up his hands.

'The publishing deal . . .' She hesitated. 'I think that you, Giovanni and I should all work on it together.'

'I think we should order a bottle of wine, Megan, you've got my head spinning with all these suggestions. I guess I've never thought of the farm as anything other than a working olive farm. Maybe we were too close to see a bigger plan.

Your suggestion is certainly worth considering,' Luca said.

'Thank you.'

'Do you think Giovanni would be interested in working on a book?' Luca frowned.

'I can think of no one better suited.'

'Could you extend your stay?'

'Well that is the big problem — my time in Italy is rapidly running out,' Megan answered with a catch in her voice.

15

After her discussion and meal with Luca, Megan sent a quick text to Giovanni wishing him goodnight, before quietly letting herself into the room she shared with Anna, unsure of what to expect.

The room seemed in the same order as when she left, and Anna lay curled up in bed under a sheet, breathing heavily as she slept soundly.

Megan changed for bed as quickly and quietly as she could and made sure the alarm was set on her phone for their early breakfast before they set out on the first day of their tour.

It felt as though she had barely closed her eyes before her phone alarm beeped her awake again, and it took her a few minutes to adjust to her surroundings. From the sound of water running she presumed that Anna had beaten her to the shower, and she smiled, relieved to think that at least her companion was up and getting ready for the day.

'Ah good, you're awake. I hope I didn't disturb you,' Anna greeted Megan as she emerged from the bathroom, fully dressed.

'No, not at all, I never heard a sound. How are you feeling today?'

'I'm feeling a lot better, thank you. I think having someone to listen made all the difference, Megan. I can't thank you enough for that, and I must have slept well because I didn't hear you come to bed.'

'No problem. Yes, you were sound asleep when I came to bed.'

'Did you really mean it when you said I could work on the articles with you?' Anna asked shyly.

'I sure did — are you still up for it?'

'Definitely. I'm going to make some notes while you're getting ready, then we can go downstairs together.'

'You don't need to wait for me. You must be hungry — go ahead without me, if you want.'

'No, I'd rather wait and go together

if that's ok.' Anna blushed. 'I feel a bit embarrassed after yesterday.'

'Well there is absolutely no need, but I do understand. I'll be as quick as I can. You get writing while you wait.'

★ ★ ★

After breakfast when everyone on the tour gathered in the foyer waiting for the coach to arrive, one of the ladies approached Anna.

'Hello, dear,' she began. 'It's lovely to see you are feeling a bit better and ready to come with us today.' She had a little gift bag in her hand. 'Now, it's not much but we had a little whip round and got you something since yours got stolen.'

Anna, startled, looked towards Megan, who gave a quick shrug to indicate she knew nothing about this but also a little nod of encouragement.

Anna opened the bag and pulled out a purse.

'It's not expensive,' the lady said quickly. 'But we knew you would need one. Open it,' she encouraged.

Anna did as she was instructed and found a twenty-euro note. She gasped.

'I couldn't possibly accept this —' she began to say.

'Of course you can,' the lady insisted. 'We want you to.'

'I don't know what to say. Thank you, thank you all of you.' Tears filled Anna's eyes as she hugged the woman. 'This is so kind of you.'

'The money is for luck,' the lady advised Anna.

'It's already working its magic,' Anna answered with a smile.

Megan turned to Luca and whispered, 'I think she's right, she's a different girl since yesterday.'

'I think we're all different since yesterday and there are a lot of people working magic,' Luca answered with a wise nod.

★　★　★

The remainder of the week flew by in a frenzy of sightseeing. They visited the

Colosseum, the Pantheon, the Catacombs and threw coins into the Trevi Fountain, all in the blazing summer heat. They sampled pizza, binged on gelato, and shopped until they dropped, or at least window shopped until their feet protested, and Megan kept all her social media followers up to date on their adventures.

Megan worked specifically on the article covering The Vatican. As cameras were forbidden inside many of the rooms, Megan needed all the skills she had acquired during the previous months to put into words the magnificence and absolute beauty of St Peter's Basilica, The Sistine Chapel and The Vatican Museums. There were moments when she felt it was all too much and found it a completely overpowering experience.

The week was exhausting, and she joked with Luca that he and Anna must have made her work harder than it normally was on her own.

The evening before they were due to leave for home, Luca invited Anna to join them on the journey home in his car.

When they had a minute on their own, Megan thanked Luca for his offer.

'No problem. She's a changed girl, even in this short time,' he answered.

'She is and she's worked so hard this week. The others on the coach adore her, and she's been a joy to be around. Who would have thought so much good would come from a bad start?'

Luca nodded in agreement.

'I hope that Claudia will give her a chance to continue with all this good work.'

'I hope so too.'

'I've spoken to Roberto about your suggestion.' Luca said.

'And what did he say?' Megan held her breath.

'He thinks it could work and wondered why we didn't think of it before. He's going to do some costings and comparisons.' Luca laughed.

Megan let out the breath she had been holding in one long sigh.

'Thank goodness for that. I was worried you would both think I was interfering.'

'The only problem is getting Giovanni on board.'

'Maybe you should call a family meeting to discuss the suggestion?'

'Or maybe we should just get you to ask?'

Megan laughed.

'Cowards, both of you. I would be happy to help you pull together ideas and examples. And I could sound Giovanni out, but could we put it on hold until I return from the UK? There are some other things I need to sort out first and I do want to have a room at Laura's to come back to. I don't want a family dispute to cause me to lose my lodgings.'

★   ★   ★

Megan and Anna presented a unified front to Claudia on the first day back in the office, where they met to discuss the Rome trip.

'I'm very pleased with how the trip ended after such a dreadful beginning,' Claudia said. 'I hope you have recovered from the incident, Anna. Our insurers have agreed to replace all you lost to the thief.'

'Thank you, but there is no need,' Anna answered. 'The bank replaced my cards, I didn't have much else in my bag and I was gifted a new purse.' She smiled.

Claudia looked taken aback at this response and Megan smiled inwardly. She imagined Claudia had prepared herself for a whingeing, petulant Anna demanding compensation for her experience.

'Right — good, then,' Claudia continued. 'I've been looking at the articles, you've both written.' Megan could feel Anna stiffen beside her as both girls held their breath. Claudia continued, 'They are good, incredibly good, great work from both of you. We have decided we are going to run with a special edition dedicated to our capital city using work from both of you, and Luca's fabulous photography.'

Anna squealed with delight and hugged Megan, much to Claudia's continued surprise.

'Thank you, Claudia,' Megan answered for them both. We are incredibly grateful.'

'You deserve it, all of you,' Claudia said, then looking at Anna, she added, 'I have a story I would like you to cover, involving the cutbacks in the culture budget and how it will affect tourism in our city. Do you think you can handle it?'

'Yes, I can.' Anna took out her notebook and began jotting down the details.

Claudia raised an eyebrow at Megan, who gave her a broad grin in reply.

Megan left them discussing plans. She had a few days to write up her additional articles for Bob, and she knew exactly where she wanted to be while she did so.

* * *

Giovanni met her when she arrived at the farm. Taking her in his arms, he whispered, 'I've missed you so much.'

She reached up to him and kissed him.

'Me too, Giovanni, I've missed you holding me like this.' Then, breaking away from him, she added, 'Work allowing, of course.'

Now the summer was upon them the olive farm was blooming and Giovanni was kept busy tending to the grove, the orchards and all his other responsibilities. The house, to Megan's delight, also took on a whole new life. No longer dark and cosy, the windows were curtained by delicate voile allowing the light to stream through, the fireplace was filled with flowers from the grove and the warm-coloured throws and cushions were replaced by textiles in bright yellows and whites.

Mama, Papa and Nonna were delighted to see her again and fussed over her, Mama and Nonna intent on feeding her constantly while Papa questioned her on her latest assignments.

By the end of the first day together, as Megan and Giovanni relaxed on the terrace at the back of the house with a glass of wine, work done and with time to talk, Giovanni raised the subject Megan was dreading.

'I don't want you to leave Italy, but I've racked my brains for a solution, and I can't seem to find one.' He stared into the distance as he spoke, unable to meet her eyes. 'But maybe I am being too forward, and you will be happy to go home.'

Megan leaned forward and took his hands in hers.

'Giovanni, I wish I could stay here. I really do. If I were to find a way to extend my stay here, would you be pleased or unhappy?'

Giovanni held her hands tight.

'Megan, I would be delighted. My heart is breaking at the thought of you leaving.'

Megan smiled. 'Those are the words I hoped to hear.' She reached over and kissed him. 'Well, before I had the accident that caused the bump to my head, Eduardo had discussed a proposal with me, but I had forgotten all about it until I

275

was in Rome and it came flooding back.'

'Go on,' Giovanni urged.

'The proposal is from a publisher who has read some of my work and wants me to consider working on some books for him, one of which is capturing the history of the olive and olive farming, and such like.'

'And have you accepted?' Giovanni asked, his face earnest. 'Would it mean you could stay in Italy for longer?'

'It would be up to Bob really — and to be honest I'm not sure whether I'm up to the task.'

'But you must make Bob agree and you must accept. I can help you with the details. Please, Megan — please consider accepting.'

'And you would help me? You could find the time?'

'I'll persuade Papa to get extra help if needed.'

'Good, because I spoke with Eduardo today and told him I would accept — but only if you were the co-writer, and Luca was the photographer.' Megan gave a mischievous smile.

Giovanni sighed with relief and then began laughing.

'You tricked me into agreeing to write a book with you.'

'Yup.'

'I love you.' Giovanni kissed her.

'I love you too,' she whispered.

'Thank you, Megan. This is something I've dreamed of for a long time, but I would never have made it happen. And now you have, and we will be working together and with Luca too, Papa will be happy.'

'I need to get Bob to agree but even if he doesn't, I can visit on weekends and holidays to get it done. We'll work it out.'

'We will.'

'Now, on the subject of Luca.' Megan took another deep breath and decided to strike while the iron was hot. 'I have another suggestion.'

There was a long silence after Megan finished outlining her suggestions of using the empty buildings, specifically with Luca and Roberto in mind.

'I can give you figures showing increased income where businesses have opened to the whole tourist experience, or utilised their empty spaces to let to creative industries or crafters which are sympathetic to the farming community,' she added.

'Do you think Luca and Roberto would be happy to live here and display their work here on the farm?'

'I think with the right marketing, they would bite your hand off for the opportunity.'

'Papa would be delighted to have both his sons working and living on the farm. I would love for my siblings to be an active part of this business which belongs to us all. I think you're right, Megan, maybe we've not been open to looking at diversifying in the tourism direction and it could save the farm for future generations.'

Megan breathed a sigh of relief.

'Will you at least consider it?'

'Do I have an option?'

'Not if you want me to come back.'

'Now I know why they call you an influencer.' Giovanni laughed as he scooped her into his arms.

16

It seemed to Megan that Giovanni and his family were on track to become even closer, which she felt delighted about, even though she knew there would still be some obstacles to overcome.

The question on her mind, though, was: could she walk away from the olive farm? Bob might agree to give her a bit more time to work on the project with Giovanni, but she knew realistically her job was based in the UK and there was no changing that situation.

If only she could come up with a solution. She could of course abandon her career and perhaps find a job working on the farm, to remain close to Giovanni, but that would put her back at square one. Was she prepared to do that?

She had worked hard these last few months and discovered a Megan she never knew existed. She needed to fight to keep that girl and her dreams alive.

Whether it was the reminder of the old Megan or the recognition of her new self, suddenly a plan began to take shape. She bit her lip as she considered her options, would her suggestion be enough to convince her editor?

★ ★ ★

'How are you, Megan? Have you recovered fully from your accident?' Bob answered Megan's telephone call.

'Yes — thank you, Bob.'

'We were all really worried, me more than anyone. I hope you can forgive me.'

'It was a bit of a shock, not just for me — but it's all sorted out now, Bob, so you're forgiven.'

'Thank goodness. Now then, I can't begin to tell you how delighted we all are with the success of your assignment. Readership is up, advertising sales are up, our social media traffic is off the chart and the board are delighted.'

'Thank you,' Megan answered, blushing.

'These figures impact on us all, Megan. They give us a bit of breathing space. So, tell me, what are your feelings on the project? How, do you think it all went from your side of the fence?'

'From my side, it has been a steep learning curve. I've had a few situations where I've needed to think quickly, act appropriately and hope I made the right decision. Overall though, Bob I've loved every minute of it and I'm so thankful to you for the experience.'

'Yes, I'm sorry about some of the breakdowns in communication.' He shook his head. 'But you coped admirably and I'm proud that you did. It justified the faith we had in you. I am so very proud of you, Megan.' He sighed. 'I just hope that on your return, you don't become frustrated to be back to the old routine.'

This was her moment. So much depended on how she presented her thoughts to Bob.

Taking a deep breath, she said, 'I'm pleased I lived up to your expectations.

As you know, I wasn't sure I was the right person for the job.'

Bob laughed. 'I remember.' Then more seriously, 'Spit it out, Megan. What's on your mind?'

And she did. She told him about Giovanni, about the publishing offer, about Anna and the turnaround in her behaviour and eventually she told him about her suggestion.

'I haven't discussed this with Claudia. I wanted to speak with you first, Bob. I would like to stay in Italy and work with Giovanni on the book. I know I could ask for a leave of absence. However, I have a proposal that might work out to everyone's advantage.'

'Go on.' Bob encouraged her.

'I would like to propose I work on a freelance basis, like Luca, while I work on the book with Giovanni. That means this office saves on my salary, and perhaps between you and Claudia, you could give Anna an opportunity to work on a similar project to the one I've just completed.'

Megan held her chin high to stop her voice breaking.

'The bottom line is you want to stay in Italy for a while longer, to work on the book project?' Bob said.

'Yes, I would like to if that would be possible.'

'Can you leave this with me to mull over? We don't want to lose you, Megan, though I fear we may have already. I also don't want you to lose out, given the work you've done for us. I want to make this work for you — we owe you that at least. Can I give you a call tomorrow if that suits?'

'Yes, that would be great. Thanks for listening, Bob.'

'No problem, Megan, and good luck — whatever happens.'

★ ★ ★

Megan was on the terrace of the apartment when the call came from Bob. She felt her mouth go dry and her hands begin to shake.

'Hello, Bob.'

'Well now. I have some news for you, which I hope will meet with your approval.'

Megan held her breath and waited for him to continue.

'I've spoken with quite a few people today, including our chief executive.' He paused. 'Here is our proposal. We don't want to lose you because your profile has lifted our readership figures and advertising income. We propose we keep you employed as a columnist, on Oyster World, and we would expect content from you every month.'

Megan couldn't believe her ears; this was her dream job.

'Claudia is more than happy to provide you with freelance work. She also wants you to write for Piccolo Mondo — she thinks very highly of you, Megan. She would also like you to act as a mentor to Anna, with a view to her being given a similar project to yours, after a probation period. So hopefully that will give you time to pursue your own writing career, while having a steady income and from our business perspective, we keep your followers on board with us.' There was a moment's hesitation. 'What do you say, Megan?'

Megan took another deep breath.

'I don't know what to say.' She felt her throat constrict as her eyes filled with tears. 'Thank you so much, Bob. This is more than I expected. I'm really grateful.'

'You deserve it, Megan. I'll email the paperwork so you can check the details, and make sure it meets your approval.'

'Thank you again.'

'Just don't forget you still have an assignment to wrap up.' He laughed. 'Now get off this phone and tell Giovanni the good news.'

'Yes, I shall, immediately, thank you.' She was already speaking to herself as Bob had rung off.

She listened as Giovanni's phone rang out. He must be out of signal range on the farm. She was deciding whether to leave a message when suddenly Giovanni answered. At the sound of his voice, the tears started to flow.

'Megan, are you OK? What has happened?' he asked, concern in his voice.

'I'm fine, Giovanni, I'm more than fine. Bob has agreed I can work from Italy.' She half laughed, half sobbed down the line.

There was silence on the other end of the phone and Megan had a moment of panic, and then she heard him sob.

'Oh, Megan, thank you for making this sacrifice. I couldn't bear to live without you. I am crying with happiness.'

'Me too.' Megan giggled. 'Oh Giovanni, are you really happy?'

'Yes, my darling. I can't wait until we start our new life together. Wait until Mama and Papa hear the news — they will be as delighted as I am. Can I tell them?'

'Yes — and give Nonna a big hug from me for pushing us together.'

Giovanni laughed. 'I will be sure to do that.'

After phoning her parents and siblings

who were delighted for her and not at all surprised, Megan jumped when her phone rang. She smiled as Luca's name lit up.

'Pronto,' she answered.

'Many congratulations. We are just never going to get rid of you, are we?' Luca teased her.

'Nope. I bet you regret being paired up with me now.' She laughed back.

'Never! You are the best thing that has happened to my brother and our family. I can't wait to get started on our project.'

'Thank you, Luca — for everything.' She smiled.

Megan looked in the mirror and for the first time she liked what she saw. Gone was the timid girl crippled with self-doubt; before her she now saw a confident woman, sure of where her journey was taking her and no longer afraid.

She congratulated herself for having the courage to speak up for what she wanted, something she would never have imagined herself doing not so long ago.

Megan looked over the view from the terrace as she and Laura enjoyed a leisurely breakfast, before she headed to her new home on the olive farm.

'I hear it's someone's birthday tomorrow,' Laura said.

Megan smiled; she thought she had kept her birthday a secret.

'It's just another birthday, nothing special.' She hated a fuss when it centred around her.

'Ah, but this will be your first Italian birthday, so that makes it special. I shall miss you when you leave, it's been nice sharing with you. Now everything is changing.' Laura pouted.

'I dare say I'll be easily replaced, by a certain professor,' Megan teased. Then more seriously she added, 'All these plans the men are making — I hope you don't feel left out of things.'

'A bit, to be honest,' Laura answered.

'You do know when Luca and Roberto open their galleries and workshops it will bring customers, tourists and suchlike?'

'Yes, I dare say it could get quite busy and like you've said before there are other events they could try like cookery, ceramics and music demonstrations, which will hopefully bring more people to the farm,' Laura agreed.

'Laura, when you say 'they,' who do you mean?'

'Them, the family.'

'And what part are you going to play? After all you are part of the family too, and I don't think for one minute think they will find as good an event coordinator as the one sitting beside me right now.'

Laura's body stiffened as she absorbed Megan's words.

'I know, Megan — they do not have the skills I have to organise events and keep them running smoothly.'

'So, what are you waiting for? Laura, you are miserable in your job. This opportunity is perfect for you and has your name written all over it.'

'I'm phoning Papa right now,' Laura laughed, picking up her phone.

* * *

Megan woke to the sun shining on her first day living on the farm. Her phone pinged, and she realised she had lots of messages wishing her a happy birthday.

She smiled, thinking it truly was a happy birthday here on the farm with Giovanni. Footsteps on the stairs alerted her and she quickly sat up as Giovanni entered the bedroom carrying a tray. She squealed with delight as she saw a steaming mug of hot tea instead of coffee, a vase with a red rose, and a plate of bacon and toast. There was also a small package beautifully wrapped in gold with a red bow.

Megan felt her heart skip a beat as she unwrapped the gift to reveal a new copy of Dante's *The Divine Comedy*.

'Thank you, Giovanni, it's beautiful.'

'Do you really think so?' Giovanni asked.

'I do. It reminds me of our first time alone together.'

'Good. I suspect we may have some

visitors shortly to give you some cards and gifts.'

'So, perhaps I should get up and showered.'

'Absolutely.'

Megan washed, dressed and smiled at Giovanni's choice of gift — so beautiful and thoughtful.

Giovanni was correct. When she made her way downstairs, it was to find Mama, Papa and Nonna waiting with cards and gifts. She was enveloped in a shower of love and good wishes. Coffee was drunk and cake provided by Mama was eaten until it was decided by Papa that the working day should begin.

As she left the main house, a car drove into the courtyard and Megan was surprised to see Anna at the wheel.

'Hi Anna, is everything OK?' Megan could feel her heart beat faster as she wondered why her colleague was at the farm.

'Yes — thank you.' Anna kissed Megan on both cheeks and gave her a hug. 'I'm sorry to turn up unannounced, and I know you are busy.' She spoke to Megan and to Giovanni who had now joined them in the yard. She paused, aware that Papa and Mama were now also watching.

'I wanted to apologise to you, Giovanni, and all the family. I'm sorry for the distress and upset I caused. This family showed me nothing but kindness when I was a little girl and I should have respected you more than I did.'

It was Papa who stepped forward, and Megan held her breath, knowing his reaction could make or break Anna.

'Anna,' he said. 'Thank you for your words. They mean a lot to the whole family. Perhaps we lost sight of the little girl who played in these very groves and for that I apologise to you. The past is gone — we can't change it, but we can build a better future.' He moved towards her and kissed her.

Megan also moved forward to hug Anna followed by Mama, who had tears in her eyes as she thanked and comforted Anna in equal measure.

Giovanni, who had held back initially,

moved towards her.

'Thank you, Anna, I hope we can all move forward now.'

Megan again held her breath, concerned at his formal tone.

'I hope so too, and I owe it to Megan who despite me being jealous and nasty towards her, saw something in me I had lost along the way.' Anna smiled gratefully.

Suddenly Giovanni;s stance relaxed and he smiled back.

'Yes, I guess she's had that effect on me too. All the best of good luck, Anna, with your new project.' He gathered her in a hug as he spoke. 'Now, folks, there is work to be done. Let us get moving.'

'Thank you for forgiving her,' Megan said to Giovanni when Anna had driven off.

'No, thank you — you made it happen. I was caught up in my own sense of importance, annoyed that Anna should dare to offend our family. We should have tried harder to understand her pain. You have made me realise that.' He reached down and kissed her.

Everyone went about their business, and Megan made her way to the office to complete the final work on her Pizza to Pisa assignment, until around lunchtime when Giovanni appeared.

'Enough work for today. It is your birthday, after all, and I have made us a picnic lunch with wine, to take down to the grove.' he announced.

Megan rose from the work desk and wrapped her arms around him.

'Thank you, Giovanni, that sounds absolutely wonderful.'

Together they made their way to the far end of the olive grove, which was bursting with olives just ready to harvest.

'I thought we could stop by the tree which won the award at the Olive Farmers Ball, the event which really brought us together,' Giovanni suggested.

Megan squeezed his arm.

'Ah Giovanni, you are an old romantic.'

'I hope so.' He smiled back.

They laid the rug over a patch of grass

and sat in the shade of the old tree. Giovanni had prepared cheese and ham panini with olives and sundried tomatoes on the side, and fresh peaches to follow, with a bottle of sparkling wine.

After they had finished eating Giovanni stood up and laid his hands upon the tree.

'This tree has sustained our family for so many years. I hope it will do the same for many more. If you look closely, you can just make out the initials of my grandparents and parents carved into the bark.'

'Really?' Megan was on her feet. 'Show me.'

Giovanni led her around the tree pointing out the initials and Megan ran her hands over them.

'Isn't it wonderful to think these will be here forever, marking their love,' she said.

'Yes, it is.' Giovanni led her around the tree.

'Oh!' Megan gasped, as she saw the newly carved initials. *GR amo MH* surrounded by a heart shape.

'Do you like it?' Giovanni asked.

'Oh, Giovanni, I love it.' Megan reached for his hands to steady herself as she felt overcome with emotion.

Then to her surprise Giovanni dropped on to one knee and reaching into his shirt pocket produced a box, a jeweller's box. He opened it to reveal a diamond solitaire nestled in a velvet cushion. Megan held her breath.

'Megan, my darling, amore mio. Will you do me the very great honour of becoming my wife?'

She clasped both hands over her mouth and her eyes filled with tears.

'Oh Giovanni, yes, yes, I will be honoured to be your wife. I love you so very much.'

'I love you, my darling.' Giovanni placed the ring on her finger. 'Thank you, amorino.'

They held each other close for a long time, reluctant to move and break the spell, until the sound of nearby workers disturbed them.

'Let's head back, Giovanni. I want to

show Mama and Papa.' Megan reached out and began to clear up.

'No rush, we can finish our wine first. They are not going anywhere. I want to keep my fiancée to myself for a little while more.' Giovanni smiled at her and she kissed him, happy in the moment.

When they reached the courtyard on their way back, it surprised Megan to see Luca's car parked there.

'Luca has come for a visit; we can tell him our good news,' Megan suggested.

'Absolutely, good timing,' Giovanni agreed.

But when Megan entered the main house it was to a chorus of *Happy Birthday*. The entrance was decorated with balloons and streamers and Megan quickly realised that not only was Luca present, Roberto, Laura and Bruno where all there, apparently to help her celebrate her birthday.

'Surprise!' everyone shouted.

Megan smiled and then gasped as her parents, sister and brother emerged from the hallway.

Giovanni held up her left hand and beamed as he shouted, 'She said yes!'

The room erupted with shouts and cheers, back slaps, kisses and hugs and amid the celebrations were Megan and Giovanni wrapped in each-others' arms. Giovanni confident enough to trust her love and no longer afraid of taking risks, and Megan sure of her own capabilities and talent, now content in the arms of the man she loved.

★ ★ ★

'Tell me again, Chloe.'

'Megan Hopkins, soon to be Rossi, it is true, today is your wedding day.'

Megan squealed and sat up in bed.

'And if you do not believe me, look at that gorgeous designer wedding dress hanging from your wardrobe. Created, I believe, by the award-winning designer Ryan Hopkins.'

'Oh Chloe, isn't it beautiful?' Megan gazed at the ballerina-length white gown, cut in a simple flared style, in satin with an overlay of organza, with a scalloped neckline of lace made by Nonna and decorated with diamante daisy-shaped flowers, with spaghetti straps and completed with a short veil embossed with delicate daisy shapes, simple but elegant, and very much in the style of Audrey Hepburn.

'Chloe, can you believe all that has happened in such a short time?'

'Yes, I can, because my sister Megan makes things happen and I am so proud of her.'

'Chloe, I do love you and also I miss all our girly chats cuddled up in bed together in the flat in the depths of winter when we were freezing.'

'Heavens, remember when we first moved in to the flat together? We could barely afford to live there, and rationed the heating. They were happy days, Megan, but now we are all grown up and you are about to get married. And you and Giovanni make the perfect couple.'

Megan smiled at her older sister.

'I think so, apart of course from Luca

and Roberto — but they are an old, married couple now.' Megan laughed. 'With two thriving new businesses and a gorgeous little daughter, Isabella Sylvianna. I just adore my little niece — I wish she could be a flower girl.'

'Now that would be a stretch when she is only three months old,' Chloe reminded her, smiling. 'But I'm sure she will make her presence known, if her Nonna ever puts her down.'

Megan laughed. 'To be fair, we are all a bit smitten with her.'

'Hello, is anyone out of bed in this house?' Laura shouted from the bottom of the stairs. 'There is a wedding to get dressed for, and since I am in charge, everything will run on time and no mistake.'

Megan and Chloe dissolved into laughter.

'Oh dear, we are in so much trouble.' Megan giggled. Then she shouted to her sister in law to be, 'It was all Chloe's fault, she's held me back. I would have been up and ready ages ago if she stopped chattering.'

Laura entered the bedroom and frowned, wagging her finger.

'You are both as bad as each other.'

'Come join us Laura.' Megan pulled back the sheet and patted for Laura to jump in.

Laura hesitated, then, laughing, she kicked of her sandals and jumped in. The three girls proceeded to spend another half an hour chattering and gossiping.

'Bruno is driving me crazy; he is taking this ushering responsibility so terribly seriously,' Laura confided.

'It wouldn't be the Bruno we know and love if he didn't. I'm sure he, Ryan and Roberto will do a fantastic job. Just like my two bridesmaids, who will be the best maids any girl could ask for.' Megan declared, wrapping her arms around them both.

'And if those maids do not get their bride out of bed and under the shower in five minutes, there will not be a wedding — well, not today anyway.' Laura jumped up, pulling Megan with her.

'I'm getting married today.' Megan clapped her hands and ran into the shower room. She thought of the loved ones joining them today — her parents, her siblings, Giovanni's family and their friends. She pictured Mama holding little Isabella and Nonna, the original influencer, looking pleased to see her first-born grandson happy at long last. Her soon to be brother in law and best friend Luca, who was their best man, and whom she had never seen happier than when he and Roberto fussed over their beautiful baby daughter. She knew she was blessed.

All week they had been busy preparing the grove for the wedding. Both Megan and Giovanni wanted the ceremony to take place in amongst the olive trees. The reception was to take place in the newly refurbished event hall, where Laura now regularly held successful exhibitions and demonstrations, located adjacent to Roberto's art gallery and Luca's studio. One of the newly refurbished houses was now home to Luca,

Roberto, and baby Isabella.

Life on the farm had changed and Mama and Papa enjoyed having all their family living and working beside them. Only Laura still chose to live with Bruno in the apartment in Verona.

Megan smiled as she remembered how she and Giovanni kept busy throughout the year, holed up for the winter months, working along with Luca on the series of books they had been commissioned to produce and which were due to be published in the next month.

Giovanni also continued to work on the farm but had expanded his work-force thanks to an unexpected increase in sales and the extra income from the events. He was happier, too, now that he was working alongside his siblings, and no longer the only one responsible for preserving the family history.

Megan continued to produce work for Bob and Claudia and she also worked on a diary based on her experiences, which was being considered for publication. Giovanni's beautiful office in the barn seemed to inspire her; maybe it was Dante and his works which had encouraged her to throw herself into her writing, maybe it was the peaceful environment, but Megan suspected it was contentment and love.

The scene was set, her bridesmaids already slowly making their way down the walkway decorated with apple blossom. As she walked through the lemon-scented grove on her father's arm, carrying a bouquet of jasmine and freesia with olive stem foliage, to meet Giovanni, her husband to be, who stood proudly looking at her with love in his eyes, Megan smiled calmly at their guests, and family.

In her newly found peace and confidence, she knew she was far removed from the girl who stood in Bob's office, who wanted to be a writer, but was terrified of the world. Now she was a woman who could speak up for herself and who could encourage others too.

She smiled lovingly at Giovanni knowing she was no longer a lone traveller; she was indeed an influencer, whose ideas and insights could help to enhance the lives of others. She was so excited to face the future, stepping forward to meet it with her wonderful husband at her side.